Ideas Above Our Station

Stories

route 18

First Published by Route
PO Box 167, Pontefract, WF8 4WW
e-mail: info@route-online.com
web: www.route-online.com

ISBN: 1 901927 28 8

Editor:
Ian Daley

Editorial Support:
Isabel Galán, Susana Galán, Roger Green,
Manuel Lafuente, Tony Maguire,
Oliver Mantell, Susan Tranter

Cover Design
Andy Campbell
www.dreamingmethods.com

Route would also like to thank
Carmen, Manolo, Alicia and Claudia in Calafell
for their hospitality during the
reading period for this book

Printed by Bookmarque, Croydon

A catalogue for this book is available from the British Library

Route is an imprint of ID Publishing
www.id-publishing.com

This book was possible thanks to support from
Arts Council England

Stories

Aubrey

Alexis Clements

There were three things that Aubrey did every time that she got home from a long day, or any day, really. First, she would switch on all of the lights in the apartment, the most important one being the long fluorescent light in the kitchen because she was convinced that fluorescent light was a sun-substitute of sorts, in as much as it was really, really bright and always made her feel more awake than all the other dull, yellowish lights in the rest of the apartment. The second thing that she did, after she had all of the lights turned on, was turn on the radio, talk radio, so that it sounded like there was someone else there with her. And the last thing that she did was to pour herself a nice, tall, stiff drink, usually with two fresh ice cubes from the freezer.

She did all three of these things before anything else; before setting down her bag, before looking at herself in the mirror, before going to the bathroom, before laying down on her bed and staring at the ceiling, and even before starting to think about what she would have for dinner. Doing these three things was very important to her, and it had been that way for at least eight years now, maybe nine, maybe longer.

***

'Hi, John. Hi, it's Aubrey. Aubrey Haltzman, from Grover Junior

High. Hi, how are you? Yeah, I know, it's been, gosh, let's see, fifteen, maybe sixteen years. Yeah. I know, I know, it wasn't easy. Actually I got your number from Suzie Tyler. You remember, Suzie, you two used to kiss in the costume room during drama class. Of course, yeah. She gave me your number. I know, it is weird isn't it? So, how are you? Doing well, I hope. Oh, you know, I just wanted to see what you were up to. Every once in a while I like to get in touch with someone I haven't seen for years and find out how they are, see how they've changed. Is that a child's voice I hear in the background? Oh, right. I'm sorry, I didn't mean to interrupt. I guess I didn't figure that this was a cell phone number. Right. Well, no, I also wouldn't have guessed that you were raising pot-bellied pigs, but that's what's so great about getting in touch with old friends. You just never know how people will have changed, and how they've stayed the same. Yeah, right, well, okay. So, I hope I get a chance to talk to you again some time. I'll tell Suzie that you said hello if I talk to her. No, not regularly. I talked to her about two months ago for the first time since I ran into her in Kentucky ten years ago. Yeah, weird, right? Okay, sure. Sounds like they're getting hungry. You must have to feed those things all the time. Pigs. Crazy. Okay. Nice to talk to you. Okay. Bye.'

***

The man at the counter had been waiting for Aubrey to give him his ticket for three full minutes. There wasn't anyone else in line behind him and none of the other ticket booths were open. Aubrey went on talking: 'People don't really appreciate the aubergine for all that it is.'

'No, I don't suppose that they do.' There was a brief pause as Aubrey sighed, and the man seized the opportunity. 'Did you have my ticket there?'

'Oh, yes, sorry. Here it is. The planetarium show starts at three, which gives you plenty of time to do a little bit of exploring before that. I recommend the exhibit on predatory insects. The poisonous beetles are particularly good.'

'Thanks.'

'Thank you for coming. Enjoy your time here, and come back soon.'

The crowd on Tuesday mornings was always a bit sparse, to say the least. In general, a rickety old natural history-cum-science museum wasn't a big draw any time of the week, but Tuesday mornings were particularly quiet, especially since the school groups had stopped coming three years ago because of an incident with the falling whalebone. But Aubrey didn't mind, she liked the museum, and liked her job there. She liked talking to people about what the museum had to offer. She liked having contact with the public. She had heard that working with the public could be a drag, but she felt it wasn't so bad. People always smiled and acted very politely, always said how interested they were in her suggestions and that they would be sure to have a look. And they often left with the feeling that they had learned something, even if they would soon forget what that was. She felt she had a purpose in the grander scheme of things, as if she was witnessing the minute shifts that took place in the universe that most people never noticed.

***

'Hello. This is Aubrey. I was hoping to get in touch with Mavis. That's right, Mavis Beechum. She was my mother's cleaning lady for about six years. No, I didn't know her, not really, but I just thought it would be nice to talk to her. Is she around? Out to the store. Oh, no, that's alright. But please, let her know that I called, and say hello from my mother. It's Aubrey Haltzman. That's my name. My mother's name is Georgiana. That's right. Will you let her know when she gets back? No, no, just let her know. Thank you. It's been nice talking to you. Okay. Bye.'

***

On her way to and from work in the mornings and evenings Aubrey preferred to take the long route, not the quick one. Every day she woke up between 7:22 and 7:27 depending on if she was dreaming or not, or if it was sunny or cloudy, or if she'd had a little bit too much to drink the night before. She took care of her morning business – getting dressed, having breakfast and all of that – and was out to the bus stop by around 8:04. Then she would wait for the bus to come, as it usually did between 8:13 and 8:26. After taking the first bus into town then she had to switch for a different bus that went out around the park, which usually took about twenty-eight minutes, and then she would catch a third bus which would take her to the taffy factory, two blocks down from the museum, getting her into work at roughly 9:38, or thereabouts. She did the same thing to get home, except in reverse. She preferred the long way to the quick. She didn't like trains very much.

The only time in eight years that she was forced to take the train was about a year and a half ago when her bus pass fell through a hole in the lining of her jacket and she had to run back home to get change, which caused her to miss her first bus, which meant that she wouldn't make the second or third buses either, and wouldn't make it into work at her usual time unless she took the train.

That day on the train she ran into Sidney. Sidney had been working for the museum when Aubrey had just started. Aubrey only got the job because a professor of hers had mistaken her for someone else, she had never made much of an impression in college. Sidney was working as a janitor there and didn't seem to make much of an impression either. She hadn't seen Sidney since starting at the museum and had never really liked talking to him.

'Andrea,' he never got her name right. 'Is that you, Andrea?'

She didn't respond to him. She held her bag tighter and tried not to make eye contact with anyone else on the train.

He stood and came closer. 'Andrea, right? I thought it was you.'

She hugged the bag tighter.

'You still working for the museum? I don't think I've ever seen you on the train before. I ride it all the time. You must be running late.'

She wondered how he knew.

'You haven't changed a bit. Are you still selling tickets? I figured you would have left that place by now, got yourself a job doing something else, at some big important place downtown, a smart girl like you.'

She looked down at his shoes.

'That old museum hasn't changed a bit since I left. I brought my grandson there a while ago and it's just the same. Don't think the new janitor's doing his job though. There were lights out in the astronomy room and dust all over the apes.'

He had on old-man shoes with Velcro instead of laces. He used to wear laces. Aubrey wished she hadn't dropped her bus pass.

'Seems like people wouldn't want to look at the same stuffed apes year after year, but they never complain, do they?'

She would sew the hole in her pocket up at lunch, sew it three times over again.

'Well, nice to see you. I've got to get off here. I'm working at the bookbindery now. I clean up all the extra bits of paper that get sliced off the edges to make the books nice and even. I like the smell of the freshly cut paper.'

Aubrey didn't look up to see him go.

That was the only time that she had missed her buses.

***

'Marjorie? Hi, Marjorie, it's Aubrey. Aubrey Haltzman. I used to come into your shop all the time. Aubrey Haltzman, you remember don't you? I used to love your shop. You do? Do you really? Yes, with the yellow ribbons, that was me. I know, ages. Ages. I looked it up in the phone book. I remembered your name from the deliveryman who used to come and you would have to spell it for him every time because he always got it wrong. Ages, I know. How are you? Oh, he did? Really? Well, I'm sorry to hear it. I'm sorry about that. I can understand. I can understand that. My gosh, that's too bad. Really. Oh, no, I keep to myself, pretty much. I work at the science museum. No, no, that's the big art museum. No, I work at the science museum. Well, then you should come visit. It's a great place. There are a lot of other things to do, that's true. I know. You know you always sold the best chocolate bars. It's true. Well, I guess they are pretty much the same. Oh, well, you had better go and take care of that. I'm so glad that I got the chance to talk to you. Okay. Bye. Bye.'

***

Sitting in the kitchen with her drink resting on the table and the radio chattering in the background, Aubrey began to carefully read over the letter that she had been working on for a while now, a few months really. She wanted the letter to be just perfect before sending it to the director of the museum. She knew it was a long shot; she knew that it wouldn't be easy to convince anyone that the aubergine deserved its very own display case, but she thought it was worth a try, at the very least.

She first had the idea for the exhibit about eight months ago, about six months after missing her bus and around the same time that she switched from regular, cheap Scotch to the expensive kind. She was in her favourite grocery store, wandering through the produce area, thinking about all the different things that she could eat in the coming week, all of the different vegetables that she could include in those meals, and one vegetable kept appearing in the back of her mind: aubergine. She had always had a certain affinity for the aubergine. It was such a nice vegetable, the deep purple colour and the thick green stem, that lovely organic shape, and the hefty feel of it in your hand. It was a significant vegetable, as opposed to a shallot, for example. A shallot, in the grand scheme of things, was a relatively insignificant vegetable. But Aubrey was never sure what to do with an aubergine, so she had never bought one.

On that particular afternoon she approached the speciality vegetable section as she normally did, carefully observing the vegetables that the ordinary shopper didn't have the time for or the interest in. Aubrey was certain that she was no ordinary shopper. She stood in front of the speciality vegetable section pondering the choices available to her, the time and skill that their individual preparations required. And as she stood there one of the produce clerks approached with a cart full of boxes. He saw her silently contemplating the food options before her and after a brief pause he said something that Aubrey couldn't quite understand, his heavy Slavic accent distorting the words.

'What was that?' she asked.

'I zed, ef you can't dezide, take ze ekkplant.'

She thanked the man for his advice and watched as he nodded and pushed his cart further down the aisle towards the apples and bananas. What an odd man, she thought, as her hand reached out and picked up the largest of the eight or so aubergines lying in a basket at the rear of the case.

When she arrived home from shopping, after having turned on all the lights and the radio, with her tall, stiff drink in hand, she took out the weighty aubergine and placed it on her cutting board. Taking a chair from the table she sat down opposite the vegetable. For roughly twenty or thirty minutes she remained there, sipping her drink, staring at her newly acquired aubergine. She hadn't had much real contact with eggplants in her past, no vast pool of experience to draw on, no insights or interesting tidbits of information. This was new for her, a new experience. She was excited, aroused even. She finished her drink as she contemplated the purple thing in front of her.

Eggplant parmesan was the only meal that she had ever heard of that featured aubergine as the main ingredient. She wasn't sure if she had ever actually eaten eggplant parmesan, but she had definitely seen it on menus in restaurants before. Pleased with the idea, she pulled from her refrigerator a half-full bottle of week-old spaghetti sauce and a faded canister of parmesan cheese. She wasn't sure exactly how it would work out, she didn't have a recipe for it, but she felt inspired, and so, into a small baking pan she placed four thick slices of aubergine, doused them in sauce and cheese, put them in the oven for as long as it took for the top of the cheese to turn golden brown.

She was disappointed with this first attempt, it tasted only of old spaghetti sauce and cheap cheese. She was dismayed to have turned a speciality vegetable into such an unspecial mess. Thus began her mission.

The science museum had a library near the back of the building, behind the boiler room/employee cafeteria. And so, during one of her lunch breaks not long after her first aubergine attempt, she made her way back to the library to do a bit of research. There was no official librarian, just an older, deaf man who kept things tidy and made sure that people didn't steal. Aubrey went over to the ancient card catalogue and began searching for a card on eggplant. Without much searching she found just the thing she was looking for, *Ode to the Aubergine*, by Sir Thomas Hancock. Taking the card with her, she walked down one of the many rows until she came to the 'H's and with the aid of a small step stool, she plucked the book from its place on the highest shelf.

Every lunch for the next month was spent poring over the pages of the book, which she unfortunately couldn't take home because of the library's strict no-borrowing policy. Each day she would leave her counter, her purple notebook in hand, find her way through the maze of corridors and displays to the old library, where she would sit, diligently taking notes on every nuance, every subtlety, everything there was to know about her beloved *solanum melongena.*

The aubergine, refined cousin to the potato, had a noble and exotic history, having travelled from deep within the Orient into the kitchens of the world despite its originally quite strong and bitter flavour. After years of careful breeding and cultivation the aubergine evolved into a much more subtle and palatable vegetable appreciated for its variety and heartiness, its density and whimsical colouring. Aubrey was sure that she had found something worthwhile, something that had a role in the grander scheme, that spoke to the heady world of science as well as to the hearts of man.

Occasionally the little library man would come around and peak over her shoulders to see what she was reading. She would have loved to tell him all of the fascinating things that she was learning, but he would not hear it.

After two solid months of rigorous study and bi-weekly attempts at various recipes Aubrey felt that she knew everything that there was to know about the aubergine. She was now, perhaps, the foremost living authority on the subject, seeing as how Sir Thomas

Hancock had died approximately one hundred and twenty-six years earlier. It was at this point that she began drafting her letter, the letter proposing that the museum devote an entire display case to the aubergine, the eggplant, *solanum melongena*. She had written seventy-three drafts of the letter before coming to what she felt was a concise, articulate, and compelling argument for the aubergine. It was a long and arduous process involving many drinks and interrupted by many calls to check up on past acquaintances.

Before sending the letter, she set it down on the kitchen counter, next to the aubergine that she would eat later that evening, poured herself yet another drink, this time without ice, and contemplated the impact that her work might have. She was seeking no glory, no fame or fortune, no international recognition like that bestowed upon her predecessor, Sir Thomas Hancock. She wanted only to inform the people of all that the aubergine was capable of, all that lay within its deep and mysterious skin. Sipping her drink, her satisfaction and anticipation grew. She was sure that the museum would accept, sure that they would see the importance of the project.

After finishing her drink she stood, placed the letter into her bag and walked to the post office.

***

'Courtney? Hi, is this Courtney? Oh, hi, I'm trying to get in touch with Courtney Schroeder. Right, Courtney S-C-H-R-O… Okay, sure. Hello. Yes I wanted to speak to Courtney. I'm an old friend of hers, from school. Not since freshman year of college. No. No,

I didn't know that. Really? Missing from home or missing from the country? Just missing. Right. No, I didn't know that. That's too bad. Right. Well, I will. Okay. Well, if you find her, I'd love to speak to her, to see what's been happening in her life, how she's changed. Right. Right. Okay. Bye.'

***

The museum took four and a half months to get back to Aubrey, a period of great anxiety for her, during which her only solace was the new aubergine soufflé that she was developing. It took them a further nine months and three quarters to actually build the display case, having hired the work out to a museum display case manufacturer in Sweden, to Aubrey's great dismay. In the months leading up to the acceptance of her idea Aubrey had spent many an evening diagramming how she thought that case should be filled, collecting swatches of fabric for the backdrop, choosing manuscript pages featuring elaborate aubergine illustrations, along with all manner of aubergine ephemera, such as the teapot in the shape of her beloved vegetable, which she found at an estate sale one Saturday morning. The best part of her design, she thought, the crowning glory, was the small garden patch which she hoped to fit inside of the case, with actual aubergines growing under specially timed lamps and padded with just the right kinds of fertilizers and nutrients. But it was all to no avail. Eventually the manufactured case was put into the museum, replacing the much older display case on states of matter.

Aubrey called everyone that she knew to come to the museum and see her beloved project realized at long last, roughly three hundred and twelve people. But most of them lived far away or had more important things to do.

***

'Your show starts at noon, which gives you just enough time to do a little bit of exploring before you have to be at the planetarium. There are some excellent displays throughout the museum, but just recently we unveiled a new display on the aubergine which is a truly fascinating look at that uncommon vegetable.'

The woman furrowed her brow. 'Aubergine?'

'Yes, ma'am. The aubergine is a multifaceted vegetable, not like any other, a real innovation in the world of cultivated foods, a subtle but captivating example of what nature and mankind are capable of achieving with much hard work and careful attention.'

'Don't you have displays on other things, like space and dinosaurs and stuff like that?'

'Certainly we have other displays, but this one is unique and quite special, I think. You'll learn something that you never knew before.'

'Why should I want to learn about aubergines?' Aubrey didn't get a chance to respond to the enormity of the question. The woman held out her hand impatiently. 'Have you got my tickets?'

'They're right here ma'am.'

'Thanks.'

'Enjoy your visit and come again.'

***

The director of the museum never sent her any kind of recognition for her work, no raise or plaque or congratulatory letter, but she was happy just to have people who visited the museum stop by and find out something new about the aubergine. She felt like it was a point of light in her life, a vital moment.

She heard from one of the museum's tour guides that a few complaint letters had been sent to the director's office regarding the fact that the states of matter display had been replaced. No one had sent any letters complimenting the new case. Aubrey liked to imagine that the people who liked the case, those who loved it as she did, were too busy cooking new aubergine recipes or trying to locate a specific variety in a grocery store in Egypt to bother writing congratulatory letters.

One man that bought tickets from Aubrey on the day of the aubergine case's unveiling said that he had been coming to the museum for years and never remembered a time when there had been a new exhibit added. He said that he liked to see the same things every time and that he wasn't sure he wanted to know anything about the aubergine. Aubrey wasn't sure how to reply to this, so she just handed him his tickets and hoped that he would come again.

It's A Hard Rain

Penny Aldred

Her husband was having an affair, sleeping with someone else, fucking another woman; it hardly mattered how she thought of it. There was betrayal.

Yet compared with the dishonesty, deceit and collusion that kept the West running the show and sod the rest, it wasn't that important. Compared with the lies being told about the bitter occupation of another country and the detention of hundreds of prisoners, it was hard to see that it mattered. At home there was misinformation about meetings running late, working weekends away to thrash out new directions in the firm, dinners with clients stretching into the early hours. So what? Compared with the way that the worth of life was measured in pounds and dollars rather than love and service, compared with this, the betrayal at home seemed trivial.

Maybe not trivial, but insignificant.

She held the evidence of his betrayal: two theatre tickets for a play she'd not seen. Crumpled in the bottom of the waste bin. Casually disposed of, he'd been careless of her seeing them. In the corner of the room, the television news announcer downloaded information into her brain.

She stared at the screen. Hand-held camera, lit by infrared giving hazy green night-time pictures, bombs screaming, people running, screaming. The reporter's voice as shaky as the camera. An ambush, men dragged out of a car and shot. Their wives following in a second car, gathered over their men's bodies, still and dead. The wives reached out, their hands touching skin still warm, stroking arms, faces. Wives saying goodbye to husbands.

She watched, perched on the arm of the settee. She smoothed out the tickets, tickets for two nights ago when he'd phoned and said he'd a report to write for the next day, he'd be late, to eat without him, not to wait up and he loved her.

She remembered him coming home, getting undressed in the dark. She clutched the duvet close to her to avoid his cold body touching hers, but still she felt the icy air striking her shoulder as he got into bed. She'd turned over, as though in her sleep.

The morning after she found the tickets as she made him coffee and toast. She stood in the kitchen, leaning against the sink, watching him eat and drink. Turned her cheek towards him for a kiss as he left, as always. Wished him a good day, closed the door. She heard the car start up, drive off, slow down at the junction, then finally speed off. She switched on breakfast television. Saw those women again. Hearing them wailing she thought, yes, maybe she could take it, this betrayal, smile at him and be thankful she still had a living husband; be glad that there weren't curfews and foreign soldiers in England, that the shops were full of food and clothes, that she had money to buy them, that her house had electricity and clean water.

There were rules, the country ran on rules. But people broke them all the time. She could survive a little transgression on her husband's part. She didn't deserve peace any more than the women on the television who had husbands brutally killed, who'd struggle to bury them where they wanted. She didn't deserve any more but she had much more. So she'd smile at her husband when he worked late, or had to go on business trips that meant staying overnight. She kept her breathing shallow so it didn't reach down to the agony. She stared at the women on the television, touched their pain instead.

They'd met, Anna and her husband, many years earlier. It might have been on a long march to Aldermaston, sleeping over in church halls, community centres. Hopeful breakfasts of coffee and toast, exchanging smiles but no words. So maybe the first time they met properly, spoke to each other, was when sitting in Trafalgar Square, each with friends but ending up squashed against each other, singing and chanting to end a war in Vietnam, arms linked to hold onto each other as the police tried to haul them away. Later, when Anna's flatmate was one of those arrested he'd gone with her to stand outside the police station in the small hours. It was a smaller crowd, the chanting and singing a bit thin. Then they'd talked.

For a while that was their lives, tearing from London to Manchester or Birmingham, protesting about a war, about the bomb, nuclear energy. 'Nuclear energie? Nein danke' asked the sticker on the back of the blue Beetle they'd bought for their first car, their first significant joint purchase. They'd fit work in between marches, meetings, producing newsletters. Work was to get money to pay the bills, but the real thing, real life, was the struggle.

That's what he said when he suggested they live together. (Not marriage, not then, that came later.) He told her how he wanted to wake up next to her each morning, come home to her in the evening. He said, 'together we can fight the good fight'. It was a statement of belief, a catechism. (What will we do? Strive to rid the world of injustice. What will help us? Our faith in truth and equality, with help from each other.) It's what she'd felt on her own, saving the world from its own excesses and greed was what her life was for and doing it with him, together, it made her stand straighter, her arm extend higher, her fist clench tighter.

They each left their houses shared with comrades, found a flat for two. Anna loved the novelty of keeping house just for them, planning meals for two, putting food in the cupboards and knowing it would be there when she returned to cook, loved the notes that he left her around the house. Between work and politics she made curtains from material from the market, she stripped furniture bought in second-hand shops. She poured rice and lentils into sweet jars, arranged them on the work surfaces in the kitchen, she made mobiles from feathers and shells and hung them in the windows. She put posters (Che Guevara and his beret, words from Gandhi, an anti-apartheid rally in London) in clip-frames and hung them in the living room. Let no one who came into their home doubt what they were about, Anna and her man.

At weekends, after meetings, marches, conferences their flat would be crowded, people sitting on the arms of chairs, on the floor, perched on tea chests. There were discussions and arguments: squatting and the housing crisis, was feminism a bourgeois deviation from the real struggle? Palestine, Rhodesia, the Soviet Union. As the words meandered through the evening into the night Anna would pull the curtains to, light candles, bring in blankets for anyone, child or adult who was sleeping. All quietly, not to disturb the debate. She'd bring in mugs of tea, home-made beer, plates stacked with toast, and then fold herself in his arms.

Birthdays came and came again. Thirty, thirty-one, thirty-two. He wanted to move to the suburbs, have more space, a garden. So they bought a house; three beds and a garage. In the living room he hung copies of famous paintings by famous artists. The posters were stacked in the attic. More birthdays, thirty-nine, forty. He was distracted by pensions and getting the stripes on the lawn right. He got promotion and wanted Mediterranean holidays in hotels with swimming pools and air conditioning. He didn't want to go to meetings to stop the war, fight the BNP, keep the local hospital open. He didn't want weekends roaming the country, sleeping in trees or tunnels, camping out to stop bypasses and runways. Forty-nine, fifty. Inside Anna didn't change; she still felt that those things were real life, those times from their youth were what counted, made them who they were, that their battling was the price they paid for their privileges. But as well as the aches in her heart over injustice and poverty, there were aches in her knees and a desire for small comforts. She conceded and they took their holidays in smart hotels, ate in fancy restaurants.

He often worked late, it was that kind of job. Until she held the tickets in her hands there'd never been suspicion of any betrayal.

The first two mornings after discovering the tickets she found herself going through his pockets, his desk. It made her miserable, sliding open drawers, taking out cheque books, bank statements, returning them just so. On the second morning she found a cheque stub made out to a dress shop in town, for one hundred and eighty pounds. She put it back, slid her arms into her woollen coat and walked through the park to the shop where she worked.

In the afternoons Anna worked in a craft shop. She sold cards, candleholders, cushion covers, embroidered pictures. She packed up orders and sent out brochures. Goods imported from India, Ethiopia, South Africa. Bought from co-operatives, fair traded.

After that she didn't want to be in the house alone, to be tempted to sneak around his things and so this became her new routine: leave early, walk through the park, sit in a café. Here she'd drink one or two lattés and read the newspaper.

In the paper she read of wars. She read of poverty, of famine, of environmental devastation. She kept her mind and her heart turned away from her husband's infidelity. She didn't wonder who the other woman was. Or when she did start to wonder, she concentrated on the women nursing their babies, walking two hours to collect contaminated water to make milk to feed their babies.

If she'd challenged him in anger, or asked him quietly, she knew he'd have rounded on her. What did it matter what he did with his time when they weren't together, what he did with his body? Is that what it boiled down to, she wondered. What he put where, whose body he touched. He'd be much cruder, more specific. Then, reducing it to that he'd recall some notion from long ago, of free love, not owning each other, certainly not each other's bodies, what they did with their bodies. She would be the unreasonable one.

He told her lies and she returned them with smiles. She spent the evenings watching the news, current affairs programmes, flicking from station to station to find the saddest stories, the cruellest injustice. Later, in bed, she lay awake, her mind racing through the evening's viewing. Her inactivity in the face of the world's disintegration appalled her. When did she stop caring? And when did the world start to fall apart? And a tiny voice asked if the two were linked.

Beside her, her husband slept. His betrayal was a blip on the surface of the world's inhumanity.

She picked up leaflets in the craftshop, read posters on the noticeboard and started going to meetings, sitting at the back, leaving before the end. She was out more. There were fewer lies at home; he didn't need to say where he was. It was distracting, seeing what was going on. One meeting, about a windfarm, or maybe about an oil spillage washing up against a vulnerable coast, someone recognised her, someone from many years ago. Anna was drawn in, started volunteering her help. She took some photocopying to the shop, did some typing at home, organised a coach, booked a meeting room, met a speaker off a train. She started to feel more at home, that she was back inside her skin, and that she had something to keep her thoughts from wandering.

That she could watch the despair of other lives and her small actions made the despair more bearable to her.

She still went to the café, read the paper. But then there'd be letters to write, to newspapers, MPs, posters to design, fundraising to organise. One day in the café, as Anna was writing to a prisoner in Zimbabwe, sending a message of solidarity, a shadow fell across the paper. She looked up; a woman was standing there.

'Can I sit here?'

'Oh?'

Anna glanced round the café at the tables, three quarters of them empty.

'You don't remember me, do you?'

'What?' Anna looked up, took her glasses off. 'Sorry, I missed what you said.'

'Anna Jenkins, isn't it? You don't remember me do you? We were at school together. Don't you recognise me?'

Anna looked at the woman. No she didn't recognise her.

'Pauline Reynolds. As was. Pauline Johnson now.'

Hazy memory. 'Oh yes.'

Pauline Johnson sat down. She talked, going through a list of girls they were at school with. She seemed to have kept in touch with half their year and know about another quarter.

'So, tell me about yourself. What you doing? Husband? Children.'

'What? Yes, a husband. No children.'

'Best way that, I say. Not that I'd be without any of mine. But if I had my chance again, you know.'

Anna smiled.

'I've three. One to each husband. Plus a couple of step ones. My sister calls me Elizabeth Taylor. On account of the husbands. Not my looks, or my money. You like another drink?' She caught the eye of the girl behind the counter. 'Two more coffees, please.' She turned back to Anna. 'And not that I'd marry any of them again. No, I'm sticking with number three. I'm the sort that makes up her mind and does it. No messing.'

'No, it makes you wonder doesn't it, the ones who stay when it's not right. Oh yes, I was talking to that Jacky Armitage. She's not happy and she puts up with I don't know what. Might have been clever at school, but she ain't clever now, I'm tellin' you. I'm going on aren't I? Hubby number three, he says I've a gob on me. Not that he minds. Sorry I'm interrupting.'

'It's alright.' Anna picked up the card and pen and dropped them into her bag. 'There, now you're not interrupting.'

Anna moved the coffee, put it in front of her and clasped the cup.

'Oh alright then. But I won't stop long. You can get on with your writing. Now you, I remember, you were into Ban the Bomb and all that stuff weren't you? Bringing petitions round about one thing or another. I sort of admired you, you know, for principles and all that, and not minding about the other girls laughing about it.'

'I didn't know anyone laughed.'

'Sorry. Not in a nasty way. I think most of us probably thought it was a good thing. But we were more interested in other stuff. Boys and clothes and music. And you were a bit earnest, weren't you?'

Anna didn't reply. She was thinking of her husband. More precisely she was thinking of her husband's mistress. She wondered if the mistress wanted to save the world, or was she interested in dresses from rather nice dress shops, and other women's husbands?

'There was the day we all fasted. Do you remember, just the one day to raise money for something or other, I forget what. Was it you that got us to do that?'

'Yes. It was to get books for a school in Tanzania.'

'Ah. So you do remember some things then. We hid chocolate bars in the cloakroom, and then sloped off at different times to eat. And you wouldn't. Do you remember? We said it didn't matter, because we'd still get the sponsor money anyway and you said…well I can't remember. What was it?'

'I'm not sure now. Probably that that wasn't the point. That we should be honest. And to be hungry for a few hours was like an act of solidarity.'

'Yes. I think that was it. I didn't get it then. And I still don't really. Doesn't help anyone else, me suffering.' She smiled at Anna. 'Unless I send them the chocolate bar I suppose.'

Anna looked at her watch. 'I must go now. Thanks for the coffee.'

She didn't wait for Pauline to reply, or turn to wave. As she went through the door she heard Pauline. 'Hey, your paper. You've left the newspaper.' She didn't pause.

She spent the next mornings in the garden with a mug of coffee and silence. She walked along crazy paving paths, bending down to touch the fat buds of daffodils waiting to open. The slugs had slimed their way up the stems and along the leaves. They'd bitten through the buds so the yellow petals showed through the green. When the flowers opened, the petals would be full of holes. She filled the wire mesh squirrel-proof bird feeder with peanuts for the blue tits and watched the squirrels eat them.

Anna stopped reading the newspaper and watching the television. She fixed her back against the bloody and tragic news. In the evenings she sat, squashed in the corner of the settee, a cushion pulled against her stomach.

She wandered through the house, running her fingers over the tables, the backs of chairs, the work surfaces in the kitchen. She was not looking for dust; she was feeling the substance of this home they had built. She picked up a dolphin, made of glass, that he'd bought in a shop near the Rialto Bridge in Venice. She picked up a figure, a woman in soap stone that she had bought from the craft shop. She held one in each hand, feeling their weight. Both heavy, both cold.

She went upstairs, and upstairs again, to the attic. She pulled the boxes away from the walls, sliding them along the floor and picking her way over and round them until she reached the corner furthest from the door. Tucked under the eaves. There were the three posters, still in their clip-frames. She found two boxes of newsletters, leaflets, typed on a manual typewriter with uneven letters and printed on a Gestetner duplicator.

Anna made a space for herself and settled her back against the golf bag he'd abandoned a few years ago. She picked out the magazines, turned the pages, read the names. Names that were so familiar. Names of people, comrades, she'd expected to be friends with for all of her life. She thought of the old age they'd expected, dreamed of, living together in the Utopia they were creating. All gone, the friends and the dreams. All that remained was a dishonest marriage and a world that was falling apart. And a beautiful house full of beautiful things.

In the evening, the silence hung around her. Nothing except the blood pulsing through her head, she could hear that. The phone rang and the answerphone clicked on. His voice, her husband. 'Sorry darling, got to stay late, again. I'll make it up to you, promise.' And, 'Me again, darling. It's a drag. I'll be back as soon as I can.'

She switched on the television. Clicked from soap to soap to soap. Watched the actors, pupils dilating with lust, retreating to pinpricks when it was done, tears and snot, laughter and spit. She pulled the cushion deeper into her flesh, her belly, breathed into that stone dead place she'd nurtured, until she recognised the pain. It wasn't for the poor and dispossessed. Not any more. It was her own.

In the morning, after her husband left for work, ('shouldn't be too late darling' whispered in her ear) she took a suitcase from the spare room, packed it with his clothes, a few books, some music. When he returned that evening, she'd tell him he was leaving.

Always Swing Upright

Sophie Hannah

I am on my way to the Isle of Wight to give a talk on the subject of happiness. I am expected to speak for fifteen to twenty minutes, and for this I will be paid four hundred pounds. I will also get my train fare reimbursed and an all-expenses-paid weekend at The Haven, which, according to the brochure, has recently added a sauna and an outdoor hot-tub to its inventory of luxury facilities. All this – the deal Dr Helmandi has offered me – makes me very happy, though I have decided not to start my talk by saying so, not because it would shock the audience (though it undoubtedly would) but because such a remark could all too easily be misconstrued as a joke.

Also, I don't know that the other nine speakers are being paid the same amount, so it might be best to avoid mentioning the specifics of my deal with Dr Helmandi. Perhaps some were offered a thousand pounds, and some nothing at all; if one or two of them aren't as famous as the rest of us, they might only be getting their travel and accommodation paid for.

In front of me on the table there is a blank sheet of A4 paper and a copy of The Haven's brochure. Every now and then, I look again at the picture of the hot-tub, its green bubbles illuminated by discreet underwater lighting. In my hand is the pen I was holding when I boarded the train and have been holding ever since, though

I still haven't written anything. I've been staring out of the window for most of the journey, at the dozens, the *hundreds*, of squat pebble-dashed houses with tiny junkyard gardens, too close to each other and to the railway line – houses I would hate to live in, which is why I find it so fascinating to look at them when I get the chance. I always wonder what kind of people choose to set up home in these cages. What makes them so different from me, that they are willing to live in such unsatisfactory conditions? You can't just say poverty and have done with it. When I was poor, I lived in a one-room flat in a shared house, with only one bathroom between six of us. But mine was a huge room – one corner of it was a round turret – and it was in a beautiful old house with a lovely well kept garden, full of all sorts of different trees. No, poverty is certainly not the answer.

The train goes into a tunnel and the houses disappear. In the suddenly-black window, I see my blank white sheet of paper. It gleams at me, and my reflection grins. I am pleased by the sight of the pristine page, as still and unmarked as the surface of an empty swimming pool.

I turn away from the window in time to see the man sitting across the aisle from me take another can of Carlsberg lager out of the torn plastic bag at his feet. It is his fourth so far, and I can see another four in the bag. Eight cans, for a two-and-a-half-hour journey; he got on the train when I did. I noticed him because of the clinking beer cans and the scratchy rustle of his carrier bag, and because he was panting and soaked in sweat. His T-shirt and hair were wet, as if he'd sprinted all the way from Jupiter to get to the station in time for the 11.05 to London.

I would have asked him if he was all right (I cannot resist trying to find out information about strangers) but he immediately pulled his mobile phone out of his pocket and rang somebody called Darren. He'd only got a few words into the conversation - 'Hiya, mate, it's Greg' - when the train set off and his phone lost its signal. He slammed it against the side of the carriage so violently that I was surprised it didn't break, and yelled 'Fucking shite! Fuck!' loud enough for everyone sitting nearby to hear. I think he was drunk even at the beginning of the journey, even before the cans of Carlsberg I saw him consume.

Two women who were sitting immediately in front of him moved, probably because of either the smell of his sweat, or his swearing, or both. I almost moved, knowing that it was what any sensible person in my position would do, but in the end I didn't because I wanted to see if he would phone Darren again. I wondered if he had something important to say; surely he must have, if he was so angry when the signal cut out. I looked at his muddy, faded trainers and his dull skin and eyes, and couldn't help speculating about what might be so urgent. Did he need drugs? That was all I could think of. After that first attempt, he didn't try to ring Darren again. He drank his beer, tapping each can rhythmically and somewhat manically with his thumb, and stared down at his lap, not once looking out of the window or at anyone else in the carriage.

I have wondered, on and off since we began our journey, why he sounded friendly and relaxed during his brief conversation with Darren – *Hiya, mate, it's Greg* – when he is clearly in a bad state of some kind. I have also been wondering if he has wondered about the empty sheet of paper in front of me, and the pen in my hand. Why, he might well be thinking, has she not written anything yet?

Once he has opened this latest can of beer and taken a swig, he produces his phone again. We are nearly at Retford; I can't imagine why he has waited so long. He punches the buttons and soon I hear him say 'Darren? Greg again. Yeah, I got cut off. I got…I was just saying, I got cut off before. So what's happening? Nothing much. Yeah, he told me. So is Steve going to be there, then? Oh, right. No, it's just that Andy said Steve was coming.'

He has an unusual face, and I try not to stare. All of his features are small, as if none wishes to be identified as the main one. Around these nondescript landmarks there seems to be an awful lot of spare face, though Greg is not overweight. On the contrary, he is tall and lanky; his large cheeks are concave, two sallow valleys.

I won't be able to watch him indefinitely without him noticing, and his conversation with Darren is becoming more tedious by the second. I turn back to my piece of paper, brushing away a hair that has fallen on to it. I don't need to start writing yet. I will postpone the preparation of my talk until the last minute, savouring the knowledge that I can easily afford to do this. I'll start when we get to Peterborough. That will give me an hour, which should be more than enough time. Then, on the train from London to Portsmouth, I will look over my notes to check that everything's in order, that I haven't missed out anything vital. I know what I think about happiness, and what I want to say about it. This will be the easiest four hundred pounds I have earned; Dr Helmandi might as well pay me to speak for fifteen minutes about my favourite holiday destinations, or what I normally have for breakfast.

'And I can say whatever I want?' I asked him, when he first rang to invite me.

'As long as it is on the subject of happiness, yes,' he said, in an accent that sounded Russian to me, though as far as I know Helmandi is not a Russian name. 'We hosted a similar symposium last year, and it was a huge success. Our participants found it extremely thought-provoking and rewarding. That is why we wish to repeat the exercise. And this time we have decided to broaden our range of speakers. Last year we asked only those who were regular tutors at The Haven. Now we want to extend our invitation more widely, to people like yourself, well-known people from all walks of life who might be too busy to facilitate a week-long course, but who can maybe spare an evening to share with our participants the fruits of their wisdom and experience.'

I assumed 'experience' was a euphemism for foolishness, since it can hardly be enlightening to hear only about the correct decisions a person has made, the bits of their life they've got right. In my opinion – and I think I could prove this if I had to – every truly wise person is also foolish. I don't mean that they started out foolish and then, having learned valuable lessons, they grew wise. Anyone who is unlucky enough to discard, permanently, his foolishness will quickly become estranged from his wisdom – the one is needed to power up the other.

I said none of this to Dr Helmandi on the telephone. Instead, I said 'Of course' and 'That sounds great', because he had mentioned, at the very beginning of our conversation, the sauna, the hot-tub and the money. I had no objection to sharing the fruits of my wisdom and experience, especially not with The Haven's clientele, who paid thousands of pounds to attend symposia on happiness. I was fairly certain that, after the weekend in question, I would return home with all my wisdom intact; the symposium's paying participants would relieve me of none of it.

I think it's safe to say that most people would not choose to share anything that they value greatly with possibly undeserving strangers, and I would not have agreed – hot-tub or no hot-tub – to give my talk if I'd imagined that the forty-odd members of the audience I'd be addressing would all end up as wise as me without having done what I'd done to achieve it, without having thought and puzzled as I have – the legwork, as it were. One of the things I have always found fascinating about giving others the benefit of my wisdom is how willfully and comprehensively they refuse to take heed. I've often felt as I imagine a prison official would feel if he unlocked the big metal gate and all the prisoners inexplicably refused to cross the threshold to freedom, opting instead to return to their reeking cells.

My thoughts are interrupted by more of Greg's swearing. 'Fucking cocksucking fuck!' he bellows, smashing his phone against the back of the seat in front of him. He's lost his connection with Darren again. A small metal object falls to the ground. 'Motherfucking fuck,' he mutters in a tone that is more moderate, picking it up. From what I can see, he seems to be trying to stick it back into the side of the phone. He presses more buttons. 'Darren? Greg. *Fuck*!' A failed attempt. His face is red with frustration. I can smell new sweat. It doesn't smell bad, like body odour. It is the clean sort of sweat smell that I associate with exercise, though in Greg's case I imagine it is the sweat of righteous fury. He feels entitled to speak to his friend Darren, and objects to the randomness of life, its lack of a proper, coherent shape. I can empathise with that, as somebody from The Haven might say.

Greg tries again, jabbing with his forefinger. I don't know how he is managing to have this effect on me, but he's actually making me feel quite tense. I am, once again, rigid in my seat, waiting to see if he'll succeed or fail. I ought not to care. Last time Greg spoke to Darren, nothing interesting was said. What does it matter to me whether someone called Steve that I don't know will or won't be attending an unspecified event?

I marvel at the contagiousness of strong feelings. Because Greg so evidently cares, I also care; watching him makes me feel a fraction of what he is feeling. I wonder if I could work this into my talk on happiness: hang around with happy people, watch them being happy, and it might rub off on you. Unless you're the sort of person who signs up for courses at The Haven, in which case observing happy people will only make you feel excluded, resentful and inferior.

'Daz? Yeah, it's me, Greg. Yeah. Fucking signal keeps going.' He chuckles, as if he hasn't, only moments ago, been crimson-faced with fury. 'Yeah. Hey? I'm on a train. I'm on a train,' he repeats. 'Yeah. That's why I keep losing the fucking signal. So Steve's not going to be there, you reckon? Right, right. It's just...I wonder why Andy told me he was coming. Yeah. Andy. I think that's what he said, anyway. Why, did he not say that to you, then? Did he not say to you Steve was coming?'

I frown. Next time Greg loses his signal, I will try to catch his eye in the hope that we might start chatting. I would really love to know why he is so rabidly determined to pursue, against the odds, a conversation that is manifestly pointless, one that should have been over within twenty seconds. Is he working up to making some crucial point? Will there be a startling change of subject that will leave poor Darren – and me – reeling?

I turn back to my blank page and write 'Happiness' in the top left hand corner and 'Sonia Coney' in the top right hand corner. I make my handwriting slightly larger than it is normally, so that Greg can read my name if he wishes to. Of course, he wishes to do no such thing, which is partly why I am someone who is paid to give talks about happiness and he is someone who flies into a spitting rage over the unavoidable interruptions to his inane ramblings.

We have not yet arrived at Peterborough, but I start writing anyway, earlier than I'd planned to; I must do something to fend off tidings of Steve and Andy, and what one might or might not have said about the other. Perhaps if Greg sees me frowning, hunched over my paper, trying to concentrate, he will move, or shut up.

'Great pleasure blah blah,' I write. 'Beautiful place, welcoming atmosphere/people etc. When Dr H rang to invite me, he said that…' I stop, put down my pen. Does it matter if I prepare my talk using a mixture of notes and properly-structured sentences? Will that be confusing? I decide that it won't. Better to do what comes naturally, and not worry about being consistent. No one will see what I've written down apart from me.

I pick up my pen. 'Never given talk about happiness before, though feel as if ought to have done – surprised Dr H first person to ask me. I'm ideally qualified, because I am a happy person. Only been miserable three or four times in entire life. Each time it was someone else's fault – cause external, not internal – and each time (imagine emotional state as Weeble wobbling but not falling down, reverting to right way up, way it's used to etc) bounced back to happiness as soon as could. (Miserable people other way round – things might fleetingly make them happy but – again like Weebles – quickly revert to natural morose, negative state.)'

God, I'm good. I love this Weeble image, and it came out of nowhere. It would be really helpful if I knew more about the science of Weeble-making. Why *do* Weebles always swing upright? Do they have magnets or lead weights in their bottoms? I turn my paper over and draw two large egg shapes. I draw a horizontal line across the middle of each one. In the first, I write 'Happiness' in the top half and 'Misery' in the bottom half. I draw a little black cylinder next to 'Misery' which is intended to represent the magnet that keeps misery below happiness. In the second egg, I put 'Misery' at the top, and the magnet in the 'Happiness' section.

I chew my pen, thinking hard. So am I saying that, in order to remain happy, one needs to make sure one's magnet is in the misery section? I smile, realising that if I stick too rigidly to the Weeble image, I'll ruin it. I turn the paper over and write, 'Make sure negative feelings are weighted down (like when drowning kittens) so that they can't surface. Make sure positive feelings always spring back up.'

Greg has lost his signal again. He hisses a sequence of obscenities, and throws his phone on the floor in disgust. It lands in the aisle, between us. I lean over to pick it up. As I hold it out to him, I say, 'Would you like to use mine?' I imagine that this might lead, somehow, to my solving the mystery of Greg. I am probably being naïve. Still, who could be happy without being naïve time and time again? The trick is to make sure you don't remain naïve about any one thing for too long.

'Cheers.' Greg holds out his hand without looking at me. When I pass him his own phone, he tosses it down onto the empty seat beside him. He holds out his hand again. This time he looks at me, but he doesn't smile. His expressionless face tells me that he is not even remotely interested in me.

I lean over to give him my phone, already regretting the offer. What if there is no mystery of Greg? He is sweaty, drunk, prone to violent rages, but it is not a mystery. 'My phone's usually pretty good on trains,' I tell him, 'but if you lose the signal, please don't smash it against anything.'

'All right,' he says, already pressing buttons. 'Andy? It's Greg. Did you? I never got no message. When was this? Oh, right. Oh, no, I must have been on the phone to Darren. Hey? No, it's not. Yeah, I'm not, I'm using someone else's phone, on the train.'

I sigh. Why did I offer him my Nokia, an expensive new one? Will it mean anything to Greg, that he has agreed in advance not to bash it against anything hard? Perhaps there is no mystery of Greg but a substantial mystery of me that needs to be solved. I write, 'One key to happiness: never finding self boring. Then will never find others (life) boring.'

I need to go to the toilet, but am reluctant to do so until Greg has given me my phone back. His conversation with Andy does not sound as if it is nearing an end. It is all about Steve: what he said, what was said to him. Andy, I assume, is supplying all the detail; Greg seems only to be responding. Either he's a bit slow or the information he's being given is confusing. I hear the fizz of another lager can opening.

Sighing, I start a new paragraph. 'Since never given a talk about happiness before, asked Dr H what sort of thing he had in mind.' I have always known that I was going to include this snippet about Dr Helmandi in my talk. And, actually, his paying clients have a right to know that the owner and manager of The Haven has a completely inside out persective on something as important as happiness. If I don't tell them, who will?

'Dr H said it was up to me what I said, how I structured the talk, from what angle I approached subject,' I write. 'I told him that I have always found an excess of freedom to be a restriction. Did he want a personal list, the things that make me happy, numbered one to ten?'

I could have done this easily: 1) my husband, 2) my children, 3) the rest of my family, 4) my close friends, 5) my work, 6) holidays that involve sun, beaches, pools and beautiful hotels, 7) having lots of money, 8) art - good books, films, music, paintings, 9) lovely meals and drinks, 10) capitalism – the fact that, three years ago, I invested a substantial amount of money that I'd saved in an equities-based fund, and now every year I get interest on that money that is more than a lot of people's salaries. My money grows into more money; I find this magical and miraculous. When I asked my financial adviser how exactly it happened, he said 'Capitalism'.

I jot down my ten favourite things, because I love making lists, especially nice jolly ones like this.

'I asked Dr Helmandi if he wanted a list of that sort,' I write beneath my top ten, 'or if he wanted me to offer advice about how other people might make themselves happy.' I realise I have lapsed into complete sentences. Maybe that's better. I can reduce it to notes on the train to Portsmouth, but for the time being, writing it out properly will help with the flow.

'Because the two would be very different animals, I explained to him. What made me happy was unlikely to work for any other individual.' This is true, I think. Stupid things make me happy. I am happy now because my phone has not yet cut out, and Greg already looks a little more relaxed, slumped in his chair with his feet up on the back of the seat in front.

'In the end, because I needed a bit of context, I asked Dr Helmandi what other people had said, the year before. What sort of talks on happiness had his last troop of eminent guests given?' I refused to use Dr Helmandi's word, celebrities, because that suggests, to me at any rate, people who are famous for no good reason. "Well," he said, "it was very interesting. They all had one thing in common, which I could never have predicted, gratifying though it was." Aha, I thought, knowing this would be something I could get my teeth into.'

I frown, then draw a line through this last sentence. By teeth, I mean my sarcastic, condemnatory, superior teeth; it would be unwise to admit that I was eager to sneer at the one thing all the happiness talks had in common before I even knew what it was. The sort of people who go to The Haven believe in a community ethos – that phrase is all over the brochure – so I probably shouldn't say that it's only slightly dim people who go around saying exactly the same things as other slightly dim people.

'Dr Helmandi said, "All the talks, without exception, focused on being, not on having or achieving. People shared how they wanted to be, the changes they felt they needed to make within themselves in order to be happy. For some, it was about becoming more spiritual. For others, it was about making more time for themselves, or slowing down a bit. Some people felt they were on the verge of burning out."'

I drop my pen, frustrated. Greg still has my phone, and my bladder is starting to feel uncomfortably full. Maybe notes would be better after all. At this rate I'm going to end up writing down every single thing Dr Helmandi said to me. I'm wasting my time if I'm hoping that my audience will be alerted, by his hackneyed use of language, to his tired and unprofitable way of thinking. Holistic types like him always put 'becoming spiritual' at one end of the scale and 'burning out' at the other, just as presenters of property programmes on television use 'living the dream' and 'getting a reality check' as their north and south poles. But who at The Haven would think of this, and draw the appropriate conclusions?

I pick up my pen again. 'Dr Helmandi dismissed having and doing in the same breath. Or rather, his previous speakers did. They all said that achieving things in the world, and having things in the world, did not make them happy. The focus of all last year's talks, according to Dr Helmandi, was internal, not external. What made the speakers feel fulfilled – the only thing that did – was being a certain way in their hearts and selves. Curiously, it was the same way for all of them: they all said they strove to be unmaterialistic, unambitious, calm, still, accepting, part of nature.' I pause, as it occurs to me that I might be describing a corpse, a dead person's way of being. A striking image, but to be on the safe side I'd better not use it. 'When they succeeded, they were happy; when they failed, they were unhappy.'

It was lucky Dr Helmandi couldn't see the expression on my face at that point in our conversation. The bloody charlatans, I thought to myself, taking The Haven's money and spouting, in exchange, the sort of new-age claptrap they imagined would please the punters. And I bet it worked, I bet all the symposium's participants fell for it. What could be more seductive – if you have poor self-esteem, if you need to pay to attend lectures on how to be happy – than hearing a lot of famous people whine about how their big houses and flash cars haven't solved any of their problems? Money, fame, having lots of people in the world who think you're fantastic, even people you don't know — all of these are things that contribute hugely to a person's happiness, and anyone who says they don't is a liar.

Deciding to let rip, I write down these last few thoughts. This is what I want to say, so this is what I will say. Dr Helmandi won't approve, but he will still have to pay me. I have the letter of agreement in my file at home, with his signature at the bottom. 'The irony,' I write, 'is that now you all think I'm a terrible, crass person.' I picture forty-odd bodies, badly dressed, cross-legged on the parquet floor in front of me. Flecked socks that look as if they're made from muesli. 'But you've got it the wrong way round. The people who say that all you have to do is be calm and still and spiritual – they're patronising you.' I decide not to name names, though I know from last year's programme who the culprits were. 'Think about it – these people are all well-known and well-off.

That's a bit of a coincidence, isn't it, when they profess not to care about worldly success? Of course they care – but they think it'll be better for you if you don't, because they believe you're not like them - you're not as good as them. They don't think you're capable of achieving anything, so they tell you the secret of happiness is not to bother trying – essentially, to give up.

'While it is of course true that if you are happy in and with yourself, it will be harder for circumstances, events and other people to rob you of your self-esteem, it is also true that if you start from a position of high self-esteem, the world's good opinion and rewards can make you feel *even better*. If you are fundamentally happy, your happiness is that much more elastic and capacious – there is no limit to how much it can grow. That's why you *should* try to achieve, that's why, if you can afford to, you should buy a beautiful house and go on holiday to a luxury beach resort in Mauritius rather than to a manky caravan park in South Wales. Aim for the better thing every time, and in every sphere of life, big and small.

'As for this distinction between being and doing – it's totally spurious. What's the point in being if you aren't going to do anything in the world? We are all grown-ups here, most of us are well over the age of eighteen.' I imagine the cross-legged bodies again; yes, they will mainly be middle-aged, and mostly women, I think. Many will recently have been abandoned by husbands or partners. 'We should have sorted out who we wanted to be a good while ago. If you haven't already done it, do it quickly, get it over with, and then you can turn your attention away from yourself and towards the outside world, and everything it has to offer.'

I've come to the end of my piece of paper. I didn't bring a second sheet with me, so I start to write on my *Daily Telegraph*. I'm gaining momentum and I don't want to stop. 'Get as much as you can out of life – love, friendship, money, fame – the works. Instead of paying through the nose to come here and get a pseudo-spiritual pat on the head from people who secretly despise you, spend your money on nice new clothes and make-up, perfume, a diamond ring, a Ferrari, throwing a brilliant party. Take unpaid leave from work and canoe across the English channel.

'Do you want to know how I know that I'm a truly happy person? It's because the only things I want, now, that I haven't got, are the luxury extras. That's because I've got the basics sorted. And to stop wanting – not to want anything any more – that's my worst nightmare and it should be yours too. So, I would quite like a team of live-in servants and a home large enough to accommodate them in rooms that are adjacent to but separate from the main house. I would like to have a twenty-five-metre heated swimming pool in my garden, and I would also like a full-time pool attendant, since I don't want to have to faff around with water filters myself.

'If all this sounds shallow and frivolous, it's only because I am already completely, utterly, happy with who I am, my way of being. Which doesn't mean I think I'm a wholly good and ideal person. On the contrary: I can be a complete bitch, as I'm sure you have no trouble imagining.' I will pause here so that they can laugh. 'But I suppose what I'm saying is that I am the best person that it's feasible for me to be, and I decided a long time ago that I wasn't going to be attempting any more unrealistic changes to myself.'

I am tempted to punch the air, so pleased am I with my little thesis. 'I've done well professionally,' I write, 'but I could still do better – and only if I surpass my previous levels of achievement, only if I out-perform myself, will I gain greater recognition, my swimming pool and servants, and greater happiness.'

I can't wait any longer to go to the toilet. Greg is still talking to Andy about Steve's likely perambulations. As I stand up, he looks at me and points at the phone, as if to remind me he's still got it. I wonder if he will keep an eye on my handbag if I leave it on my seat. I decide not to take the risk, but I point at my notes and The Haven's brochure and whisper 'Mind these for me?'

He gives me a thumbs-up. I grab my bag and walk to the toilet, smiling. So far this journey has been very productive. I have written my talk, and Greg and I have reached an amicable understanding.

I wash my hands with a small round lavender soap I have brought from home (because train soap is always so foul) and dry them on my jumper because there are no paper towels and I don't want to touch the filthy cloth towel that dangles from its holder like a baby's sagging nappy.

I return to the carriage and blink several times, looking quickly left and right, like a character from an absurd cartoon. Greg isn't there. My papers have gone – there is nothing on my seat or on the table. And his plastic bag full of beer cans is gone too. He's stolen my talk on happiness, and my phone. The *bastard*. I can't believe it. Why would he do that? Why? Notes for a talk on happiness have no street value. It makes no sense.

I vow to hunt him down, which will be easy, as he must still be on the train. I know this route very well, know that there have been no stops since Greg's theft of my possessions. I march in the direction of the buffet in search of a member of staff, but find myself walking into the toilet again, the same one I've just left. Once the door is locked, I burst into tears. I can't let anyone see me like this. Greg has deliberately stolen my things. He's a savage; that was clear from the start. I should have moved, sat somewhere else. Anyone else would have. I've always been the biggest idiot I know.

Greg is still on the train, which means there is a chance we will see one another again, and I won't risk him seeing me with tears streaming down my face. Now that he's done this to me, the only way I can play it is to pretend I don't care. Maybe I'll pretend it was some sort of trap – that I wanted him to steal my possessions in order to prove some theory I was working on, for my talk. Something about the lower orders.

Oh, God, my talk. I think about the notes I made, my stolen diatribe, and realize there is no way I can say those things to those people. Just because I believe it doesn't mean I can say it.

Has Greg read my notes?

Once I've stopped crying, I cover the red blotches on my face with concealer and unlock the toilet door. I see the ticket inspector at the far end of my carriage, and start to walk towards him, but I never get that far. I am stopped by a sight that I find even more surprising than what I am already describing to myself as Greg's strange and motiveless betrayal of me. My things are back on the table, including my phone, and Greg is back in his seat. His carrier bag – now empty, for he is on to his last can of beer – is at his feet.

'Where…you…?'

'Cheers,' he says, as if there is nothing wrong. 'What do I owe you for the call?'

'You took my things away,' I say. 'I thought you'd stolen them.'

He looks at me as if I am crazy. 'I went to the bog,' he says. 'I took your stuff with me, so no one'd nab it. You told me to keep an eye on it.'

'Oh.' I can't think of anything to say.

'How can I keep an eye if I'm in the bog? So I took it with me.'

'Thank you.' I sit down and turn my face away from him. I feel as if I might cry again, and that would be embarrassing. He was looking after my things more conscientiously than I would ever have expected him to. But why hadn't he waited until I got back? I was less than five minutes; he could have waited. Didn't he anticipate my coming back and being worried? The issue is not resolved, at least not as far as I am concerned.

'Are you that woman?' Greg asks.

I could say, 'Depends which woman you mean' but I can't be bothered. I say yes.

'I read what you wrote about happiness,' he says. 'On the bog.'

I look at him. 'And? What did you think?'

'Thought it was good.'

'Thanks,' I say.

'Do you really want a swimming pool and servants?'

I tell him that I do.

'Reckon you'll get it? Ever?'

'I've no idea,' I say sharply. Secretly, I am certain that I will one day, but I don't want to appear presumptuous.

A few seconds later I hear a papery rustling sound. When I turn to look at Greg, he's holding out a twenty-pound note. 'You can make money grow into more money, right?'

'Well, not personally...'

'Take this, stick it in whatever you've got your money in. You seem to be doing okay.'

Oh, *Christ*. 'I can't...Look, there's no...' I stop myself, because I don't want to hurt his feelings. He guarded my happiness notes, after all. 'If you want to invest, you might need a bit more than twenty quid,' I try to sound helpful. 'Most fund managers...'

'Just put it wherever your money is,' he insists. There is a funny glint in his eye that tells me he won't like it if I refuse again.

I take the twenty-pound note; there is no time to think of an alternative course of action. He smiles. 'Nice one,' he says. His phone rings, making me jump. I assumed it was broken. 'Alright, Daz,' he says, and settles into his seat for another sparkling exchange with his charismatic friend.

How the hell am I going to get out of this? Greg can't force me to take his money. I must give it back to him, as soon as he gets off the phone.

His face changes quickly, and at first I assume the signal's gone again. 'You're *joking*,' Greg says. 'Oh, man, you're joking me, please, you've got to be. Oh, fucking hell. *Fuck*!' He snaps his phone shut and looks at me. 'Give us that paper,' he says, nodding at my happiness notes. 'And a pen.' Why is it that unreasonable requests expressed urgently fare so much better than ones delivered in an ordinary tone of voice? I do as I am told. Greg scribbles something that I can't immediately read, because he is writing over my writing. He has started to sweat again, and drops are falling on to the paper. 'That's my number,' he says. 'When the twenty quid's five hundred – no, a thousand quid, get in touch, okay? And I'll meet you somewhere and get it. If I'm fucking still alive,' he mutters. 'And if I'm not, fuck it. Keep it. I'd rather you had it than anyone else.'

If this is true, it is astonishing. 'Why?' I ask, but Greg has already disappeared. I see him bounding through the next carriage. I get up to follow him, but the train is stopping. I know he will get off, and I know that I can't. I mean, maybe I could, but…no, I *can't*.

I return to my seat, more agitated than I can remember ever having been before. I must do something. I gasp as I remember my phone, then, with wobbly fingers, pick it up and dial the last dialled number. After four rings, a man answers. He says, 'Yo.'

'Andy?'

'Who's this?'

'I'm the person whose phone Greg was using when he rang you before.'

There is a lot of loud breathing before he says, 'What do you want?'

'I…look, this is going to sound odd, but…I think Greg might be in some sort of trouble.'

Andy guffaws at this. 'Greg's a dead man,' he says.

A chill spreads through me. 'What? What are you talking about? Look, what's going on?'

'I don't want to get into it. It's nothing to do with me.'

'Does he…does he owe someone money or something?'

'Just a bit,' says Andy.

'How much?'

'He owes Steve six hundred quid.'

'Is that all?' I snap. So Andy, Steve, Darren and Greg are four grown men who make a huge fuss about nothing; knowing this enables me to deal with the matter more swiftly. I no longer feel nervous. 'Look, if *I* give Steve the money, will he leave Greg alone?'

'You? You're going to give Steve the six hundred? Don't take the piss, lady.'

'Listen,' I say firmly. If this is only about money, I can handle it, no problem. 'I think Greg was supposed to be getting some money from Darren. Is that right?'

'Yeah.' Andy sounds puzzled.

'And he was supposed to be meeting someone in London and giving them the money?' I guess.

'Right.'

'Was it Steve who he was supposed to be meeting?'

Andy chuckles. 'Right. Like Steve'd turn up himself. He'll send someone.'

'Fine,' I say. 'Tell him to send that someone to the Piccadilly Gallery on Dover Street, near Green Park tube – near The Ritz. I'll meet him or her there at…' – I glance at my watch – '…three o'clock, and I'll have six hundred quid in cash.'

'From Greg?'

'Yes.' I lower my voice. 'Tell whoever Steve sends that they must say 'Helmandi' before I'll give them the money.'

'Hell-what?'

'Helmandi. H-E-L-M-A-N-D-I.'

'Got it,' says Andy after a few seconds.

'And after you get the money, you won't be hassling Greg again, will you?'

'Not unless he runs up any more debts.'

'He won't,' I say with certainty. Am I starting to enjoy this conversation? I appear to have more power than Andy, which is gratifying, even though I know nothing about him and will never speak to him again.

'If you're a no-show, Greg's a dead man.'

'Why wouldn't I turn up? I'm the one who suggested the arrangement.'

Once Andy has hung up on me, I start writing a text message to Greg. 'I will meet and pay Steve,' I write, but that looks ridiculous. One by one, I delete the letters. What the hell can I say? 'You don't need to worry, I've taken care of your debt to Steve'? That also sounds absurd. Greg wouldn't believe me; he'd think it was a trap. I stare at his number, scrawled in biro on my *Daily Telegraph*.

I sigh. I will have to see him in person, explain. But what if he doesn't agree to meet me? Presumably he will hear, eventually, that Steve is no longer after him, that some mysterious woman handed over some cash in an art gallery. But will he? My impression is that his cohorts' communication skills leave rather a lot to be desired. Oh, for goodness sake, this is insane. I have to text Greg and say something. Or ring him.

First, though, I need to ring The Haven and explain that I'm going to be late. My talk isn't until tomorrow morning. All I will miss is some of the improvised jazz, and very probably the vegetarian supper; isn't it funny how things work out for the best? Maybe I'll have tea at The Ritz, after I've dealt with stupid, petty Steve. I dial The Haven's number and ask for Dr Helmandi. 'Sonia!' he says, sounding warm and reassuring. 'We are very much looking forward to welcoming you here.'

'I'm very much looking forward to coming,' I tell him. And I am, although I will have to start from scratch with my talk. I don't want to antagonize anyone, which means I can't sneer at Dr Helmandi and the other speakers, or praise capitalism. But thanks to Greg and everything that's happened, I know exactly what I'm going to say instead.

Reading Into

Adam Byfield

'love is the peak and the pit
but nothing lies between'
George Hinckley, San Francisco, July 1968

Leaning back against the cold red brick, Jess watched yet another set of scarlet tail lights recede into the night. Checking her watch she saw that she had been stood in the chilled darkness now for... three...two...one...seventeen minutes. With a sigh she reflected that while this was twelve minutes more than she had told her friends she would be, it had only been two since she had last checked.

As a fine and misty rain began to settle about her person, she reminded herself that this was just the way it went. Rule number one in any drug deal: everything you hear is a lie. The dealer says he'll be there in five, but that was...eighteen minutes ago. Returning her hand to her coat pocket Jess continued to recall the events of the evening, in particular the drunken lecture she had delivered in the pub.

She had grown tired of repeatedly having to defend her decision made earlier in the day, to quit her regular job. Several times she had explained that she had read a lot about her new chosen direction and that she felt confident, but that was not all she had been reading. Eventually Jess had launched into a daytime talk show style confession of personal inspiration. She had briefly described the life's work of George Hinckley before passionately embarking on the subject of his death.

Hinckley had been a writer who had travelled all over the world in the late sixties researching a new book. One year, almost to the day, after he started writing the book he was in a hotel in San Francisco when he received a telegram telling him that his wife and newborn child had been killed in a traffic accident. Pausing only to scrawl a two-line suicide note on the hotel room wall, Hinckley threw himself from the window of his room and fell to his death three floors below.

At this point she had paused for dramatic effect. However, Mick had interceded. 'Well that's all very interesting, but what's some dead hippy got to do with you quitting your job?' Laughter had exploded around them and its echoes traced across Jess's lips for a moment in an involuntary smile before she realised she was not alone in the street. A middle-aged woman, whose expression appeared as heavy as her coat, had appeared and was about to pass Jess.

Dropping the smile, Jess automatically launched into her 'non-suspicious' body language. Looking up and down the street, looking at her watch and tutting. *I am certainly not loitering here suspiciously. I am quite obviously waiting to meet a friend who is late,* she seemed to say. The older woman didn't even acknowledge Jess's existence as she passed in a cloud of perfume.

Leaning back against the wall once more Jess returned to the pub. She had told them how Hinckley had written, 'love is the pit and peak, and there's nothing in between,' on the wall. Glazed eyes shone blankly back at her through the smoke and noise of the pub. Mick drew breath to speak. The point was, she had said, beating Mick to it, that it was worth pursuing your dreams because even if they fail it's better than not trying at all.

For once it was possible to see the stars and Jess looked up to them as if hoping to see Hinckley waving back. It seemed to her that he must have seen everything so clearly in that last instant and that his expression of that clarity backed up the radical change to her life's priorities that she had so recently made. All at once the future seemed to loom up before her like the high-speed sunrise of some awesome new star.

Her dealer pulled over and dipped his lights. Jess approached the car, fingering the small roll of bank notes in her coat pocket. Five minutes later she was reclaiming her place on the sofa and amid the various conversations. Looking around her friends it occurred to her, accompanied by another smile, that while they may not be at a peak, they were definitely way above nothing.

***

They had been back at his flat for almost twenty minutes when David remembered the files. Lisa was in the bathroom and he had just poured them both a drink when he caught sight of the multicoloured files stacked on his desk in the bedroom. Staring over at the bathroom door he listened intently for a moment before placing the drinks carefully on the coffee table and sprinting into the bedroom.

He had been in such a rush to meet Lisa earlier on that he had forgotten to clear away the numerous papers and files that formed the focus of his hobby. David began to heave the folders up onto the top of his wardrobe, starting with the largest first. These were the thickest files and looked to be the oldest as the names sported by their spines were faded. Kennedy, Lennon, King, Kennedy again and X were all hastily consigned to the shadowy heights, the rest following swiftly.

The last file was in his hand when he heard Lisa behind him. 'Here you are, I wondered where you'd gone. I've brought our drinks through…What's that?' David looked at the bright red file that now seemed to match his hand, caught as he was.

'It's my hobby,' the words stumbling from his lips, 'I was just putting it away.' He cringed slightly as he saw intrigue flash in Lisa's eyes.

'Oh, right.' Lisa smiled as David waited for the inevitable. 'So what's your hobby then?'

The two-word answer sat at the tip of his tongue awaiting orders as dread settled into his stomach along with the expensive dinner and red wine.

'Conspiracy theories,' he said finally, his voice thick with defeat.

'Oh,' Lisa sipped her drink and considered this. 'Like the Kennedy assassination?'

Even though the wardrobe sat behind him, in that instant David thought he could somehow see that fat black file sitting smugly under the others. 'Yeah, it's only a hobby, I'm not crazy or paranoid or anything.' They both laughed a little too loudly before falling silent again.

'So what's in there then?' Lisa asked. David realised he was still holding the slim red folder.

'Oh, this is a guy called George Hinckley. I've been reading up on him recently and I've made some pretty interesting discoveries.' As he spoke he watched Lisa sit down on the edge of the bed and kick off her shoes. She was listening to every word but commanded his gaze utterly.

'Really,' she smiled. 'Like what?'

David settled a little further up the bed with the file between them. As he explained the circumstances surrounding Hinckley's apparent suicide he flicked through photocopies of news clippings on the story. Lisa seemed moved by the tale and commented on the tragedy of Hinckley's loss when David turned to the fuzzy black and white photo of Mrs Hinckley and child.

By the time David reached the photo of Hinckley's blanket-covered body he was in full swing, eager to introduce Lisa to his recent achievements. The distance of the body from the building, he told her, was unusual. Had Hinckley simply jumped from the window he should have landed on or near the pavement. He had in fact fallen into the middle of the road, meaning he must have either taken a running leap or been thrown from the window.

David let this hang until Lisa asked why anyone would want to throw Hinckley out of a third-storey window.

'The book,' was David's triumphant answer. Hinckley had in fact completed his book and was in San Francisco to discuss publishing, David claimed. The book was, apparently, subversive in the extreme and contained information that could not be allowed into the public domain. This book would start revolutions, bring about the end of the 'square' world and lead to some kind of hippy Utopia, or so the story went.

Hinckley knew that the powers that be were about to move against him and so left a message detailing the whereabouts of the manuscript. Excitedly David turned to the next page which featured various lists of numbers.

'I thought the message was a suicide note about life without love being nothing, or something,' Lisa said. David was about to speak when he felt Lisa's hand land gently on the nape of his neck. He leant over the file that they were both supposed to be studying and attempted to continue as if nothing had happened.

'It depends how you read it,' David said quietly, his joy at sharing his work now coupled with the thrill of Lisa's touch. Hinckley was concerned about that amount of time he had spent away from his family over the previous year, he explained. Hinckley's message was unusual for him as it lacked punctuation. David had mused that perhaps this was because the number of characters in the message was important. Counting carefully, David had noticed that the message was made up of exactly fifty-two characters.

'Forty-three,' Lisa corrected after a moment, frowning, 'there are forty-three letters in the message.'

Hinckley, David continued gleefully, always used a typewriter and so would have counted spaces as characters as they required a keystroke. For the same reason the end of a line did not count. He found that putting his case before another human made it sound somehow different. For the first time he noticed how tenuous this first step sounded. This doubt was pushed aside though because David knew what was to come.

He folded out a home-made calendar that ran from mid 1967-1968. The calendar was split into weeks each of which listed Hinckley's location that week. 'Fifty-two characters, fifty-two weeks,' David said, suddenly aware of just how good Lisa smelled as she shifted to look at the calendar more closely.

His mouth suddenly dry, he went on to explain that he had numbered the considered weeks and then listed those Hinckley had spent with his family to produce a sequence of numbers.

6, 7, 11, 19, 22, 27, 31, 34, 36, 44, 48

Using these numbers to pick out letters from Hinckley's message, starting with the sixth character, then the seventh etc. David had found another message, a secret message.

love is the peak and the pit
but nothing lies between

'So what's the secret David?' Lisa asked, her eyes huge, David simply pointed to the page unable to speak.

i, s, e, n, t, i, t, t, o, h, s, t

'Who's HST?' Lisa returned her gaze to him and leaned across the file.

'Hunter S Thompson, the only person Hinckley thought he could trust to protect the manuscript. Of course Thompson denies ever having heard of Hinckley or the book.'

'The *Fear and Loathing in Las Vegas* guy?' David could feel Lisa's breath.

'Yeah,' he let the page drop.

'I love that movie,' she whispered.

'Me too,' he managed to answer as their lips met.

The file fell from the bed as if imitating the death it detailed within. It landed with a clatter and ejected its contents across the floor creating new coincidences as it went and David missed them, every one.

***

Leonard gripped his slim leather satchel with sweaty hands and fumed. He had spent the last three hours sitting in the same leather armchair waiting to be seen. As he reread the same framed film posters for the hundredth time he asked one of the several questions that continued to bounce around his balding head.

Why ask him to come in at ten if they weren't going to be able to see him until after one? Why not just ask him to come in at one, or two, or whenever the fuck they were going to get round to seeing him. Taking a deep breath he reminded himself that he must keep a tight rein on his temper today. Today was a once in a lifetime opportunity, a chance to bring his masterpiece to life. Exhaling, he cursed his stupid invisible breath, knowing that one simple cigarette could make this process just that little bit easier. He was reflecting on how unjust it was that not even this one small concession was allowed him when he heard his name.

Before he knew it he had crossed the room and entered the office in which he now found himself. Two men and a woman faced him across a wide desk and introduced themselves. By the time he had slid the heavy manuscript from his satchel he had forgotten all three names. He noticed that his hand was shaking slightly as the older of the two men started to speak.

'Hey Leonard, glad you could make it. We've had a look at the screenplay and we want you to know that we're all very excited about this project.' The man smiled hard as Leonard's heart quickened slightly. He was still digesting these words as the woman took up the thread.

'We feel that, at this stage in production,' she left this to hang for a moment, 'it's advisable for us all to put our heads together and make sure that we're all agreed on our vision for the project.'

'We like the screenplay,' the younger man volunteered.

'Oh, yes,' the others agreed, nodding and smiling.

'It's great…' he continued.

'Really great,' added the older man, still grinning.

'And this is a great studio…' the younger man paused. After a second Leonard recognised this gap as being his to fill and nodded vigorously.

'That's why we're so excited about the project,' the woman's smile showed no signs of flagging.

'Just as a great screenplay requires…deserves the best resources and skilled professionals, a great studio has needs of its own,' the older man's face was a picture of fairness.

'We feel that to make this dream a reality it needs to grow, to gain another dimension,' the younger man somehow managing to sound even more enthused than before.

'It seems to me that the strength of this project lies in its subtlety, and because of this we need to give it a hook, a pull, just to catch the attention, grab the eye. Once we get their attention this little baby will carry itself.' The older man arranged his eyebrows to appear wise above a grandfather smile as he patted his copy of the manuscript.

'Now this guy George, he was away from his family a lot…' The woman adopted a very serious expression, Leonard suddenly felt that things were about to happen. 'That must have been hard for him.'

'It was,' Leonard agreed, glad at last to hear some real confirmation that this wasn't some kind of mistake.

'And of course this was in the swinging sixties, drugs, free love…' the younger man seemed to be making excuses for something but Leonard didn't know what it was.

'The temptation must have been there for him, yet there's no real mention of either in the screenplay,' the older man seemed genuinely puzzled.

'Hinckley was devoted to his wife, there was never any suggestion that he was unfaithful and as…' Leonard's uncertain explanation was interrupted.

'So we don't know for sure that he didn't, it just makes sense to have some more direct love interest,' the younger man shrugged and all three nodded. Leonard opened his mouth to object but the woman turned back to him.

'You were about to tell us about Hinckley's drug habit,' the serious look again.

'Drug habit?' Leonard frowned, 'Well he used cannabis…' The three nodded.

'Often the way it starts…' the old man alternated to shaking his head. For a moment Leonard saw the three of them as some absurd modern art installation, nodding, shaking and smiling. Once more Leonard recognised the meaning of the silence between them.

'That's it,' he said with a shrug, turning the silence back to face the three. The pause gave Leonard time to remember that he was already annoyed and to realise that he didn't like where this *discussion* seemed to be headed.

After looking at each other briefly the three shrugged and returned their attention to Leonard. The older man spoke first, 'Now, the closing scene. Wow, very powerful, very moving, very…' he seemed to be unsure how to continue.

'Dark,' suggested the woman.

'Dark! Exactly. We were thinking that perhaps it didn't have to be quite as dark as it is; that perhaps a very slight lightening up of that final scene could really help the project as a whole.'

'Hinckley killed himself when he heard that his wife and newborn child had been killed in a car wreck. How do you lighten that up?' Leonard heard the tone in his voice but didn't regret it. The younger man responded defensively.

'Hey now, we know that the final scene is not entirely a happy one…' Leonard huffed but the woman cut in.

'It's just one aspect,' she assured him. 'At the end of the final scene we see George throw himself from the window. Now obviously this has to do with him finding out about his wife and child…'

'Terrible, terrible…' the older man shook his head.

'Driven crazy with grief he wants nothing more than to be reunited with them, obviously we understand that, that's great...' the younger man flashed the smile again.

'It's the monologue. George kind of sounds like he's given up on love not just life.'

'Given up on life we understand.'

'Of course, under the circumstances.'

'But giving up on love? That won't sit too well with the audience, Leonard.'

Leonard had closed his eyes and let the relentless words flow over him. At the mention of his name and during the pause that followed, he opened his eyes and sat forward in his chair.

'Love is the peak and the pit, but no thing lies between.' The three looked at him expectantly, blinking. 'That's what Hinckley wrote on the wall before he jumped.' The three looked relieved and nodded to one another. Leonard continued, still in a measured voice.

'He was saying that we are all slaves to love. We live in either deluded euphoria or doomed despair because of love. Love had ultimately brought Hinckley nothing but pain and as he died he cursed love with his final words. *That* is the story of George Hinckley and that is the only story I'm interested in telling.'

With this Leonard leapt to his feet, violently forced his screenplay into his satchel and stormed from the office, through that room and out into the real world; his and George Hinckley's world, he thought.

***

George Hinckley walked slowly back to his hotel room, watching the bright sun sparkle between the branches and leaves of trees. He had had an enjoyable lunch with an old school friend, followed by a couple of hours of conversation. Just before George had left they had been discussing love in a philosophical and slightly drunken manner, and it was this subject that George continued to ponder as he approached the hotel lobby.

Ever since the topic had arisen at the café George had entertained the most extreme frustration. Years ago he had written a short essay on love which had culminated, as all his essays had at that point, in a simple, yet slightly cryptic, slogan. These words, he had felt, summed up perfectly his ideas concerning love. With a knowing smile he had reached back into his mind to pluck this beautifully efficient phrase from his memory to find it missing.

Irritated, he snatched the telegram and his key from the porter and stormed into the stairwell. As he climbed the stairs he racked his brains. What the hell was it? Love is a…but there is nothing… Padding down the carpeted corridor to his room he clicked his tongue as he continued to wrestle with his memory.

George slammed the door behind him and immediately opened all the windows fully. Sitting on the edge of the bed he opened the telegram absently as he stared at the blank wall before him. He cast his eyes down to read the telegram but saw no letters as, in a flash, the golden phrase fell from his lips.

He breathed the eleven words over and over, a desperate mantra to try and combat the fraying that had already begun. Tiny slivers of gold were slipping away, back into the dark recesses of his mind, as his eyes tore about the room looking for paper and pen. Turning, he spied a pen laid just to the side of the bed but still no paper. Actually growling his frustration, George dropping the telegram onto the bedside table, snatched up the pen and attacked the wall.

'Love is the pit and the peak' at this point he reached the mirror and so continued beneath, 'but nothing lies between' He sat back on his elbows and let out a satisfied sigh of relief. At that moment the air itself seemed to echo his sigh as a gust of wind flowed coolly through the room.

The telegram fluttered for a moment, as if being tickled lightly on its underside, before leaping from the table and swooping across the room. Instinctively George sprang from the bed to catch the fast moving slip of paper. It flitted just beyond his reach as it approached the open window and so focussed upon it was he that he didn't noticed his bathrobe heaped on the floor. Tripping over the damp towelling George lunged forward and felt the paper come within his grasp as he fell headlong through the window.

What a ridiculous way to die he thought as he cleared the windowsill. From there to ground he thought only of Anna and Josie. A second later and George Hinckley lay still and silent, his empty eyes staring through the unread telegram he still clasped before him.

Taxi Driver

M Y Alam

When I first hit these roads, I was itching to scrap with every other fare. If it wasn't one thing, it was another. Didn't like the turn of my wheel, the bounce to my ride, the clothes on my back or the bass in my voice. Nothing but a piece of shit cabbie with only money on my mind: charge too much, drive too fast but still manage to take too long in getting them where they want to be. Every fare stepping into your ride can take one kind of liberty or another: chat some shit, damage the trim, piss on the floor or chip without coughing for the miles. Driving a minicab wouldn't be so bad if it wasn't for all the arseholes out there. You shrug your shoulders, grow yourself a thick old skin and you learn to live with it.

I pick up in Headingley to drop in Hunslet. Tall but scrawny looking, despite the all-round shave. Tracksuit, trainers, tats on his hands – spider web on one, snake coiled around a sword on the other. Real fidgety kind, acting like he's been on intravenous caffeine for the last week, continually scratching at his scab-covered neck and face, glancing at his snide Rolex timepiece: more wired than the National Grid. Get to the last Give Way before journey's end and in one quick and fluid movement – belt off, latch pulled, door open – the itchy son of a bitch has bolted on me, whatever abuse his imagination can conjure up trailing behind him as he scrams round the corner. David Copperfield isn't this quick. I imagine giving a vague kind of chase but that'll mean turning around which isn't so easy on a road so narrow; more so with a gearshift that hasn't found reverse once in the last four months. Besides, I don't have the energy. What's more, don't want to face the risk, considering what happened to Luckman four nights ago. Better to lose a fiver than an eye to a strung-out junkie packing a rusty blade up his sleeve.

Don't usually get runners in the middle of the week. Like everything else that's lousy about this line of work, I put it down as experience. Thing is, and no matter how long you've been cabbing, you can never tell when it comes to fares even though you know any and all travellers are capable of being a pain in the arse, especially on a night. After a while, you begin to see them with a Government Health Warning stuck on their foreheads the moment you spot them but now and then, you can't help but to let one slip through. It's nice to be nice but when you are, you tend to get it slapped right back in your face.

Nights I don't mind too much. During the day, things are a bit safer but you've got busier roads to cut through and there's an even greater army of drivers out there. Working moonlight hours, it's got a kind of a rhythm to it. I don't know so much about anyone else, but for a guy like me who's got nothing or no one during the day, working nights is the one thing that probably keeps me sane.

Back at base, a driver called Ten, and Tab, the operator, are looking up at the box, perched on a chipboard shelf with more angle than the loan shark outfit next door. It's an old black and white portable set – lousy picture, crackly sound – but they're engrossed all the same. As soon as I step up to get a better fix on the screen the picture turns to snow and the sound to a hiss. In unison, they tell me to *move the fuck out the way*. I head toward the coffee machine but keep watching the screen now that sound and image are back with us.

Most times it's either fake tits and fat arses or professional pundits and their fantasy football that grabs the attention but this night, it's something else. Some news programme by the looks of it. A few people sat on designer chairs and one guy – the presenter most likely – sat separately, asking some shit or other. The camera cuts to an Asian looking guy. Beard, glasses, smock covering him up to the neck – some kind of cleric or holy man, maybe. Not exactly what the integration mafia would dig, but it's still a free country; free enough for folks to wear what the hell they want. Hell, Friday nights you got all these damned students wearing all manner of creepy garb; flares and platforms and other bright and psychedelic bullshit. No one seems to mind about them let alone the ones with painted pallor and black everything else including fishnet stockings, stacked heels, super-straight hair, shiny lipstick, and shinier nail polish – and that's just the blokes.

The holy man opens his mouth and starts talking even more shit than the presenter. This guy seems pissed off – firing on more cylinders than he's got. Within a few seconds, he's got himself real worked up. Ranting. Unhinged. Maybe, I'm thinking, maybe he's one of us. Then again, maybe not – maybe he's one of those crazy A-rabs you keep hearing about. Either way, there's no relief because he's there as a Muslim – to present his point of view which is ready to be taken as a widely held one. Could be I'm wrong but his performance looks bad and sounds a hell of a lot worse. Just what we need, another loony tunes pissing oil all over the flames.

'It's shit,' says Tab. 'This is so fucking shit, you know that.'

Ten, one of a few older drivers that I don't know too well, seems just as annoyed:

'Typical,' he says. 'But what do you expect? These fools, they find them, give them a platform and make us all look bad.'

'Bastards,' says Tab. 'Fuckers do it on purpose.'

The presenter asks someone else to come in and respond. It's a middle-aged looking guy but he seems okay: grey suit, a greying beard and a nice pair of cufflinks occasionally sparkling off the studio lights. He seems moderate. Calm, rational and peaceful. Hell, when he starts to speak, the man seems intelligent. As one, we breath a mental sigh of relief.

'This is more like it,' says Tab. 'This guy's alright.'

'Better than the maniac,' agrees Ten.

As the man with the mind gets into his flow, the holier than thou loony tunes pipes in and starts having a go, calling him a sell-out, a hypocrite and not a proper Muslim. The presenter asks Loony Tunes to shut up but he's not listening. Keeps going on and on. For the next few minutes, the other people on the panel try getting in their tuppence worth but Loony Tunes won't let them. Some young Muslim woman, scarf on her head, Oxbridge education under her belt and middle-class upbringing coming out of her mouth tries speaking over him but he's not having it for a second.

'Fuckinell,' says Tab. 'This is a joke, man.'

'But without being funny,' adds Ten.

Sitting opposite the mad and not so mad Muslims is a local MP woman. Skinny, tall, grey haired and more self righteous than a reformed smoker, she tells him off, rude motherfucker that he is.

'She's a right racist bitch, this one,' says Tab. 'Always moaning on about thick pakis and that.'

'I was reading about her,' says Ten. 'I call her Enoch Powell in a skirt.'

'Only she's older and uglier,' chips in Tab.

Ten looks at Tab with surprise.

'How do you know who Enoch Powell is?'

'Was,' says Tab. 'Old fucker died a while ago. Gave him a state funeral and everything, didn't they? Funny that, innit?'

I never figured Tab for anything other than what he looks to be: young punk wallowing in the fact that he's had little or no schooling to speak of. Should be doing something else – a proper job, maybe studying even – but not whiling the nights away as a pissant taxi operator. Only things I ever seen him express an interest in are his ten years-old Bimmer, his growing collection of bling and *biatches*. Seems I was wrong but that's okay. Hell, wish I was wrong about all the other Tabs I see kicking around, too.

'You hear that? You hear what that bitch just said?'

'I missed it,' I say. 'What she say?'

'Don't believe I heard it,' says Tab, shaking his head, looking shocked to hell and back.

'She said it,' nods Ten, gravely. 'Got some nerve, this one.'

'What's she said?'

Tab takes a breath, looks at me like a doctor about to hit me with some cancer or other and says:

'My Muslims. She said, *My Muslims. My* Muslims? Where the fuck does she get off? *Her* Muslims? Since when was she made Caliph?'

'She said *My Muslims*?' I find myself asking. 'She didn't say that, did she?'

'That's exactly what she said.'

All I can manage is:

'But –'

'*My Muslims* as in *my niggers* as in *I'm the plantation mistress around here and I own you stupid motherfuckers*.'

I walk away, not wanting to see or hear no more, and flop on to the old settee that's been there more years than even the longest serving driver. Can't deal with this thing no more. A done but bum deal and me, I'm more than happy to be the first to fold. Some of the other drivers go on about the state of things all the time. To them, and maybe even to me, there are lots of smaller parts that make up this one big thing, whatever the hell it's supposed to be. All I know is I'm not playing any more.

My next pick up comes a few minutes past midnight. A couple, in their late thirties/early forties, on the tail end of a night out. Surprise-surprise, they've gone and overdone it with the booze. Seems to me most people overdo it when it comes to the booze. She's not as bad as him, though: on her way to being pissed, not quite there. Him, poor fat bastard's close to being out on his feet and the thing on his head – lamest wig I ever seen – is all over the place. Looking like he does, he's still got the presence of mind to slur me something about Horsforth and *none of your guided tours, either, pal* as he crawls into the back. As she helps him in, she laughs that laugh I've a heard a million times from a million other Donnas, Claires, Martines and Jeanettes. Little black/white/red/electric blue dresses with matching fuck-me shoes, tanned legs, Jimmy Saville jewellery clanking around, blonde streaks and make-up done specially, this is the high point of the week. But it's only Tuesday so it's got to be some other cause for celebration: birthday is odds-on favourite followed closely by wedding anniversary. And what a night it is: half a pound of food, too many yards of piss to count, a line or ten of dancing and then, to round it all off, a drunken, soon to be forgotten five-mile ride home in the back of some Sabu's cab whose name they'll ask but never recall fully: Karim, Kesser, Khan: *I call 'em all Tony/Sam/Pete, me – can't be arsed with messing around with them names they got.* Curry, pub, club and then home in a four-wheeled tub. The experience is no more memorable than a wet fart but it's the ritual and the routine that can't be done without.

She gets in the front, turns round and sees him slouched, fast asleep, dribbling and drooling over his dark brown knee-length leather. Shakes her head and says:

'Three pints and a couple of shorts and he's anyone's, him.'

I force a smile, slip into first, and as we set off, I ask: 'Horsforth, you said?'

'Mind you, he's not as bad as me, if you know what I mean,' she adds, drawing a little closer.

I can tell she's looking, hoping for a reaction of sorts. Any second now, she'll lean closer still and whisper a bunch of sweet fuckalls in my ear and give my thigh a bit of a squeeze if she's feeling particularly bold. She's pretty enough, trim and healthy looking but she's not sober. Right now, she's not herself and all this will be forgotten tomorrow. Besides, I'm not desperate and I'm not stupid, either – lay a finger on a fare and it's assault; go any further with a female and it's attempted rape. So she can bring it on all she likes while her stupid, unknowing, probably un-caring fat fuck of a husband snores away in the back. This fish, he's not biting and won't be reeled in, least not this night.

I pull up outside number 17 of a quiet cul-de-sac. Jack, her husband, is barely conscious and his hairpiece has slipped off completely. His wife puts it back on his head and slaps his flabby cheeks a couple of times. He moans but doesn't come round. He might be happy where he is but I'm not. Great. So I'm now forced to help this sweaty, smelly and pissed-up idiot out of my car so I can get on with my life. He stands but then collapses, his arse landing squarely on the pavement. Must have hurt but I forgot, he's pissed which is why he starts laughing. Rather than telling him to shut up, she starts laughing as well. If I worked for free, I'd leave them there.

After slapping him around some more, we get him up again. Slowly, we half-walk/half-drag him along the path and into the house. She keeps cursing at him but he's not registering a word. Every now and then he laughs for no apparent reason but that's about it. With one arm round her neck, the other around mine, eyes closed, mouth occasionally blurting and mumbling something that not even he fully understands, wreaking of bitter or whatever it is that he calls his poison, I'm surprised he can move at all. Can't see the point of it, myself; getting so pissed that you've disabled yourself for the night. Then again, maybe that is the point.

We get inside the house. White wedding day pictures along the hall from twenty-odd years ago. The happy couple – her in puffy white gown, a Bonnie Tyler hairdo and loud make-up; him looking like a toned down New Wave Romantic in a grey suit and red tie, both from Top Man or maybe Burton's. Best man with a few twinkles in his eye, standing in line to kiss the bride and maybe to get off with a bridesmaid later; both sets of mums and dads radiating pride; nippers in suits, dresses and shiny shoes pissing around and sneaking sips of Tetley's, Lambrusco and Three Barrels. Everyone smiling, everyone drinking and everyone thinking things are good and will only get better. Further on, evidence of a family; a daughter and then two sons. All blonde-haired, blue-eyed. Could be real little bastards but they look innocent enough, the way all kids do in those production line school portraits. Red school jumpers and dodgy school ties, cloudy blue backgrounds and those big smiles hiding the things that cause them to lose sleep every other night: bullying, spelling tests, the wrong trainers.

She helps him up the stairs and comes back down less than a minute later.

'Thanks ever so much,' she says, trying to sound husky and seductive.

'No problem,' I tell her. 'Do you need a receipt or owt?'

'Oh no,' she says. 'Can I get you a drink or…'

'I'm fine, ta. Nice of you but… you know, work to do.'

She tips me a few quid and I'm gone. I know lots of drivers, especially the ones with more vanity than plastic surgery junkies, who jump at this kind of chance. Quite a few got women on the side who they met this way: hard-up wives fancying something a bit more exotic than the usual whatever's on offer. That kind of messing around, it comes back and bites you right in the arse when you least expect it.

Five o'clock in the morning and I'm on my way back to Bradford, maybe stop by the Sweet Centre on Lumb Lane and catch some breakfast before I hit home and tuck myself in for a good day's sleep. Could murder a portion and a half of *channa puri* right now but then I hear Tab call out this one job a few times. They've all gone deaf or, more likely, they're all ignoring it. Council house in Chapeltown to a pool hall in Headingley then to drop at a second-hand car lot in Beeston. The fare's been waiting a good twenty minutes already.

'I'll take it if no one else will, Tab.'

'Watch yourself.'

Not many – barely any – pick up black guys. Soul brothers, they've got this reputation. One thing a driver doesn't need is a fare who's sure to make it hard work – it's just asking for trouble. Don't like paying the full fare, talk a lot of shit, show you disrespect and as soon as they get in they make like they own your car, your home and your right to earn a living. Thing is, they're not the only ones. In one way or another, every punter has what it takes to draw out and make more intense this agony we call life. Myself, I'm not fussed. Come one, come all: they're all losers as far as I'm concerned. Young and old, black and white, men, women and children are treated with equal contempt. Well, it's only fair, considering that's what they seem to have for me.

He leaves the door to the house open and gets in. You don't see so many of them, these days. An old time Rasta – greying beard, dreads gathered in a hat and a great big spliff – six skinner at least – parked in the side of his mouth.

'Right, Lalla?'

Mostly, you take the shit. You take the shit because life's too short to get all pent up about petty things like this. But it's gone five o'clock in the morning, I'm tired, I'm hungry and I'm doing this guy a favour and yet, he's got the nerve to call me *Lalla*?

'My name's not Lalla, man.'

Dread smiles, exhales a rich cloud of smoke and nods like he's some wise old fuck with a million years of philosophy drifting out his nostrils.

'No offence, my friend. Just a word is all.'

'Just a word,' I sigh to myself and stop myself from saying, *so's nigger, motherfucker*.

Dread takes a phone call and chats into his hand for maybe five minutes or so. When his conversation finishes, he turns to me, and picks up where we left off.

'What's your name, man?'

'Why you ask?'

'No reason. Nothing wrong with taking a man's name.'

'Depends what you do with it once you've took it.'

Dread laughs again.

'A man's name's a precious thing. Gives you meaning.'

'Everything has meaning.'

He gets a text on his phone but ignores it, choosing instead to hit me with more of whatever's on his mind.

'So tell me, Mister: how's things these days?' he asks.

'These days?'

'Yeah, man. You know, with all the noises about your people.'

I know where this is going and although I don't really want to find myself there, there's not much I can do to steer it elsewhere.

'What kind of noises we talking about?'

Nine out of ten sober fares will ask you, at some point in the journey, about 'things these days'. It's become a routine, for them doing the asking and for those doing the answering. It's more than the idle chit-chat people feel obliged to make when in the company of strangers – the weather, the football, the latest inane scandal taking up too much space in the newspapers or on the box. This has become real enough for everyone to have thoughts, questions and answers about.

'The terror noise, Mister. You know what I'm talking about.'

'Oh,' I say, forcing a smile, like I didn't know, 'you mean that.'

'Yes, that, man. What you think about it?'

'Why you asking?'

He gently pulls on his spliff and holds for a good fifteen seconds. As he exhales, he says:

'I'm curious, you understand.'

I shrug, make a face that's supposed to show I'm giving it serious consideration and offer him my usual response; one that means nothing, not even to me. With as much gravity as I can muster, I tell him:

'Well, it's bad.'

Dread shakes his head – part-amused, part-disappointed.

'Bad? Bad how?'

Most people don't bother asking – either because they take my first answer how they want to take it or because they're too scared to push further in case I'm one of them. Hell, four days worth of stubble, a body borne of a brown-tinted gene pool and a badge that says a name they all hear but don't know is more than enough to get lots of people feeling a little uneasy. This war and this enemy is everywhere: coming to a take-away, corner shop and cabbie near you, soon. Right now, this is just another pain we're all getting used to.

We pull up outside the pool hall in Headingley.

'Five minutes, Mister,' says Dread, and hands me a twenty before I can even think about asking him for the running fare.

'Your meter,' I tell him.

Good to his word, he's back after a few ticks of the indicator.

'Beeston,' he says. 'Take it slowly, though. I got plenty time on my hands.'

I coast along easy enough, trying to time my driving so I hit every set of lights at red.

'Bad how?' he asks again.

It's difficult being honest about this kind of thing. If you're honest, it half-sounds like you're not that far off what they're likely to think you are anyway. Unless you say *them there terrorists are a bunch of crazy inhumane and insane motherfuckers*, you all but invite them to think you're strapping a rucksack. So you got to play it careful. You might want to but you just can't tell people it's all fucked up, out of all proportion, complicated, political and economic. People just don't want to hear that. All they want to know is which side you're on: with us or against us, condemn them or condemn yourself. When you don't really know what each side is really about, it's hard to give them something so easy and simple. All you can do is bluff your way through and try to stay safe with shit like:

'It's bad. You know, for innocent people and that, it's bad.'

Innocent people are there to be fucked up no matter what. That's their role in the world and maybe it's always been that way. Even in peace, the innocent get it up the arse and then some. Why should war – a real or an imaginary one – make things any easier for them sorry bastards? Since when do the innocent have a right to be not fucked over? Hell, being all innocent like that, they're practically asking for it.

'I bet that's what you tell everyone,' he says. 'Be honest, Mister. I can take your truth.'

'Truth? You think I'm lying?'

Like a man about to administer a cure, he closes his eyes and seems to meditate for a few moments.

'Let me tell you a truth seen by me, Mister,' he says. 'And then you can think better about telling me one of yours.'

'Shoot.'

I get onto Dewsbury Road and head further into Beeston. Place was like something out of a movie that July. Half the streets cordoned off, the rest swarming with coppers drafted in from all over the place: long live overtime; all hail time and a half. There was even talk that the army was on standby. Bomb squad, forensics, DIs, DSs and even humble PCs on highly strung alert. No stone left unturned and no suspect allowed to slip through. If you matched the profile, you were stopped, searched and moved on. Might seem fucked up but for us cabbies, it was like all our Eids, Christmases, Divalis and Hanukahs had come at once. The police had one kind of presence, the journalists another. Like politicians and writers, they're all the same: arrogance personified. Even the ones going against the grain are defined by their Volvo politics, Harvey Nichols' lifestyles and bullshit-tinted memories; *wasn't Thatcher a bitch and weren't The Smiths something else.* For all the hypocrisy, they were welcomed with open arms by us all. Not only did these twats interrupt the monotony and drudge of every-day life, they helped pay for it, too. Throwing money around like it meant nothing to them – information, viewpoints, stories – if you had any of it, you were in profit before they could even clunk click themselves in. Journalists, I got to realise, are a lot like junkies – getting high off other people's realities, reduced to rattling without.

'You know this thing that's playing on the news, on the tip of the lowliest and mightiest tongue – is a Godsend for us people. That's the truth. Your curse is my blessing, Mister.'

He doesn't need to explain but maybe Dread figures it's impolite not to.

'Since it started, you know how much pressure been taken off us? It's like a nigger's never been a mugger, pimp or yardie. These days, I'm whiter than the single mothers, glue sniffers and granny rapists, man.'

Can't deny his thinking. There's a new bad and mad man on the loose and this one transcends the easy distinction of colour. Yesterday's devil might have stolen jobs, houses and women, but at least he spoke the same language, ate the same meat and wore the same clothes. This one's completely different; more alien than another life form. If that's not bad enough, this new devil has a different way of believing in and dealing with God.

'Question is, Mister,' says Dread, 'how's it feel to be like the me of yesterday?'

He's not gloating or nothing. Just stating a fact.

'Can't say I feel anything much. Like everything else, you learn to live with it.'

Dread laughs and tells me:

'You learn to live despite it. But you know what, Mister?'

The sound of the Rizla crackles as he takes another leisurely draw. With smoke trickling out of his mouth, he whispers: 'It's all fuckry.'

For the next ten minutes, he talks some more. I listen, nod in agreement when the need arises but don't say much more. No point being an echo.

I pull up alongside the patch of spare land being used as a second-hand car lot. A Portakabin in one corner and a handful of cars – mostly heaps – lined up with prices slapped on the windscreens. Dread asks me for a damage report and I tell him we're square – the twenty covers it, more or less. Maybe it's Dread's side of the conversation or maybe it's the potency of his herb that's done it, but I don't feel so tired anymore. His philosophy – if that's what it is – is different to the crap I've grown to detest more than the runners, the back seat pukers and the front seat jivers. This man's got wisdom and I'm glad he shared some of it. Hell, I almost feel bad for keeping his money; maybe I'm the one who should be paying him for being such a break from the usual.

As Dread gets out, I notice a familiar figure walking towards us. Same tracky and trainers but he's changed since the few long hours since we last met. Something's working through his veins; lead in his pencil frame keeping him straight and tall. For a moment, I think perhaps him and Dread are breaking something down together but he walks past my cab, on his way to make another raise before the sun comes up: break and enter, smash and grab, wheel and deal.

As Dread meanders over to the Portakabin, Tab's voice comes on the radio shouting another job. It's getting close to dawn and I think about taking it for a second but it's not for me, not right now. Instead, I stay parked up by the car lot for a few more clicks of the clock, looking in my rear-view mirror – the crackhead with the rash and the tats now slowly becoming a dark blob. Was a time, I recall, when I'd be itching to scrap every other fare but experience breeds resignation. It's the way of things; you know there's no point trying to make a difference: there'll always be thieves, there'll always be wars and there'll always be, without any doubt at all, the innocent ready, waiting but not so willing to feel the effects.

I check the rear-view mirror again and can still just about see him; a speck, if that. I see myself giving a less vague kind of chase this time. Nothing but a straight line between him and me. Seems I got the energy and as for the hazard, maybe it's doesn't translate into such a risk after all. Luckman lost his eye four nights ago but that's Luckman. Sure, miles better to lose a fiver than an eye but sometimes, the devil gets the better of the argument.

I dip the clutch and the gearshift, cured for a moment, locks into reverse like it was meant to be.

The Dress

Charlie Cottrell

I am one of life's hoarders. My too small Clapham flat is crowded from floor to ceiling with heteroclitaire cupboards, boxes and files containing every letter I have ever received, every cinema ticket, a breadcrumb trail of matchbooks and a thousand half-finished notepads.

I like my clutter. Each drawer-full is a collection of memories; a bus ticket from a first date I didn't want to end; the McDonalds spoon from a bitter location shoot in Scotland; shells from a world of beaches. They are the uncompiled scrapbook of my life, my wanderer's life. And in the nomadic world of a photographer, jetting off at a moment's notice and living out of suitcases and lobby bars, they are steady. Solid and familiar.

Where I like my clutter, other people do not like it. My girlfriend does not. She despises the stacked up shoe boxes and dusty box files whose magnetic clasps have retired long ago and who expel their contents in hostile protest at the first sign of movement. Her flat, her old flat, looked as though it had been lifted, complete, from Heals' window. It comprised uniform wooden cupboards with brushed aluminium handles and accessories aligned in neat trios in accordance with contemporary rules on interior design. Dust dared not settle in my girlfriend's old flat. Instead it migrated to mine where it could rest undisturbed between back issues of *Black and*

White and vintage copies of *The Face*.

'What have you kept these for?' she says holding a fistful of textless tickets before me in dismay. 'They're all faded.' They are. To the untrained eye they are indistinguishable from all the other pieces of paper debris that have failed to escape the cull but I could look at every one and give you its history. I know that the shiny one with the creased down corner was REM in Paris (November 1994) and that the pink tinged one was a Patti Smith gig in North London when I was twenty-one and in love with a girl called Isobel. I let her banish these into the rubbish pile without argument because I love her and love is about compromise. Her compromise is to move from her Heals haven into my magpie's nest. Mine is to sit in silence as all these familiar friends are raked through by hostile hands and presented to me coldly for validation: Yes that little wooden figure is creepy – no I don't suppose I need it. The pace she can work at is alarming. I would rather do this alone and give myself time to revisit the memories of this lifetime of souvenirs but it is this sentimental nostalgia that got me here in the first place. It is good to move on. It is good to remember that we can discard an object and keep a memory.

'What on earth is this?' Ah. If someone had asked me what had happened to this I suppose I would have remembered I had it though I doubt that I had set eyes on it in twenty years. As we look at it my girlfriend thinks it is an old net curtain (which it is) and I think it is a dress (which it also is). I suppose it might be described, kindly, as a punked-up tutu. It has lost some of its edge. My girlfriend pulls it out of the musty hatbox to where I had banished it years before. As she does, a crumpled photograph falls from the folds. I reach to catch it but she has it first. Her face contorts into that look of distaste we reserve especially for the discovery of evidence of a loved one's former loves. 'What the hell is this? Some sort of shrine?' She is spitting. She throws the picture to me and fingers the dress as she might a tramp's nappy. I look at the picture. Tanis looks back at me. Her eyes bright and holding the memories of a thousand secrets. The offending dress clings to her slender body like an affectionate lover.

Tanis was the first woman I had ever photographed. We were nineteen, consumed by lust and ambition and had stumbled into each other during the now foggy period of week-long parties and bedsit living of my fledgeling career. I had taken her home one night to my shabby room (the hallmarks of the hoarder were present even then) and she had stayed there for nearly eight months, pottering about the place between castings like an exquisite pet and posing for portfolio shots that I would continue to use long after she was gone. We might have been in love, it wasn't really important. What mattered was that we were in belief. I believed that she would be swept away by a soulful artist as his muse, she believed that my prolific pictures had insight and depth. We would tell each other this over paupers' meals of baked beans and mackerel, feeding each other from the same plate in our tiny attic room and keeping each other's dreams a reality. In my hands, looking up from the crumpled yellow picture, her face brought me back to a time of nervous uncertainty and the terrifying freedom of beginning.

The dress had been her idea. A new outfit for another faceless party. 'That curtain would make a great dress,' she had said. She was probably drunk, we usually were. Alcohol coursed through our veins continually since there was very little to absorb it.

'It would make a great dress,' and she had taken it down and bleached it in the bath, treading it like a viticulturist treads grapes. When it was dry she wrapped it, tight, around her little torso and had me pin up the excess as a skirt in big, irregular swathes. It looked like a Miss Haversham bridesmaid's dress, filthed up by the honey limbs that extended from it and the just distinguishable pair of pink knickers that she wore underneath. She could do that. She could take something mundane and make it brilliant. That night, in my beaten net curtain she had owned the room. I had spent the entire evening waiting to get her home. I snapped her when we had staggered back, tired and wasted from another killer evening. She was flopped over the arm of my battered sofa-bed grinning at me with the happy exhaustion of a shared evening. Her baby-white hair had fallen out of its pigtails and her ribs showed through the big holes in the net. You can see this in the picture.

I know why my girlfriend is jealous. Tanis was beautiful. A tousled angel who looks out from her portrait and knows me. To my girlfriend, to the world, she looks as perfect and as carefree as models always do in pictures. It is my job to make sure they do, no matter what is happening out of shot. Just to the left of Tanis was a skirting board that a large and fearless rat had chewed through. We could hear it gnawing away as we lay in bed. It terrified Tanis and made her cling to me in a way that satisfied my desire to appear manly. The rat hole is out of frame. My girlfriend does not see it, she sees a beautiful girl making a curtain look fabulous.

A photographer likes to play God. Through my lens I preserve the world I want to see and discard anything which might taint it. I create small scenes of perfection. Stolen glimpses of exquisite creatures. Pretty girls in crazy dresses. It is my job to make women look at them as my girlfriend now looks at the picture of Tanis. Untouchable perfection. Two-dimensional images of one-dimensional lives. We do not present a narrative, we merely suggest a moment to our audience and let them create a history. Looking at Tanis' picture and Tanis' dress my girlfriend thinks she has uncovered a secret but she knows as little about the woman she sees as I did the day I looked down through the lens and captured her. She does not know, as I did not know, the wealth of sadness behind that pretty face. She would not expect to discover, as I did not expect to discover, that the lithe body she is envying would be found in a studio in Milan, as limp and useless as a broken umbrella. Nor would she wish to learn, as I did not wish to learn, that on the very day that this smiling, knowing picture was taken, the carefree, exquisite Tanis had been told that she had less than a year left to inspire jealousy and lust in those that beheld her. To my girlfriend she is a beautiful ghost in a shabby home-made dress.

'So, do we need this?' she asks me holding the old curtain on the extremes of her fingertips. And there it is, before me, as close as it was when I scooped it up, with Tanis inside it, and nuzzled my face into the warmth of her body. As close as it was when I tried to drink in the last of her scent through tears that would not dry on the flight home from Italy. Hanging from my girlfriend's angry fingers as it had hung from my angry fingers, both of us hating it for the memory of the girl it had hugged. The object but not the memory.

Do we need it? No. We don't.

Middle Spirit

Michael Nath

We had one thing left to eat, a tortilla in a long bread roll, which I now produced from our food bag. In turns, we took bites, my wife with vivacious expression. Her face was freckled from the Easter sun. Over Surrey the clouds were high. Was I glad to be back under them.

To the right, another train from the south stretched itself along beside us, obscuring the sky. Involuntarily, I felt the competition. It was the lengthening that did it. Only we could be going where we were going. We had our destination. How could anything else be converging on it? Louise passed the sandwich to me. The train from the south lengthened further, snouting ahead, carriages empty. I carefully bit off the penultimate eighth of the egg and potato omelette so as to leave my wife something interesting; another carriage passed. Its occupant had bright blond hair in a ponytail. Then his train contracted and fell behind us. When I looked back at Louise, she winked vivaciously. She'd enjoyed her holiday. Clouds refilled the horizon.

At Victoria, we discussed taxis. 'This time of evening,' Louise said, 'the tube'll be just as quick.' We took the District Line to Earl's Court.

The carriage was pretty empty. I stood by the door to keep an eye on the cases while Louise occupied herself with a book which she'd started too late. On the opposite side of the carriage, some feet away from her, sat our blond competitor. Was I surprised? I could have been. Rather massively fit, of quick heavy build, still he sat, eyes on nothing. I saw him as a housebreaker; Brighton was his base.

No. He was too steady, martial – too big for windows. I saw him in a free-style martial arts bout, kicking and punching steadily from his quick mass. He was some kind of bum. He'd crossed the skies to get here. From one of the hot white places of the earth: Australia, South Africa – Zimbabwe maybe. His tan was resinous: hurt your finger to tap it. A surfer or a climber, that's what he was: he moved consummately when he had to; otherwise, he would stay dead still. Now he raised his eyes to the long map of stations above the carriage window. His eyes were sky grey. It was nearly our own station. I began to arrange the luggage.

At home we opened the mail, listened to the messages, did some unpacking. Louise filled the washing machine and it started to rumble. I wondered how the house had been in our absence. Still, silent, unoccupied – of course. But strange to think of. If only we could have caught it out in its emptiness, just before our own incoming, how would it seem?

While we were abroad, what materialized? At first there and gone, a pale-fringed floater crossing the eyes. As time condensed in the empty house, manifesting itself like a jellyfish; slowly firming, more glassy now, like a bottle in a pond; and next behold it turning humanoid, bronze-tinted, gold, white, grey, veiny: sitting down with the TV controller, putting the kettle –

'What are you laughing about?' Louise was standing in the doorway of the living room, hands on hips. She believes I'm peculiar. I think she compliments herself on it. Her friends' men are straightforward.

'Ah – the house.'

'What's funny about it?' she enquired gladly.

'The quality of the air.'

She retired humming to herself. After a while, she called from the other room. If I was ready, we could go round to Tesco Metro to buy things for the fridge and a bottle of bleach, which we needed.

Our road is long, straight and wide. You could run a good race down it. One hundred and seventy yards or so it must be. Light fills it, bright yellow, or when the clouds heave in from the west, bright grey-white light such as falls on cliff-paths. Outside Hotel Arden, two world travellers were smoking on the step: a chubby guy with a white 'Mission Impossible' T-shirt and green shorts, a girl with small eyes. Up above on the balcony, two girls had come out of a bedroom, one of them to iron; there was a green can of Heineken Export on the parapet. They shouted down to the smokers, and the smokers stayed put; then stepped onto the street from under the balcony:

'Lisa's gonna come down on a bungee!' yelled the ironer above.

'What?'

'Lisa's gonna come down on a bungee *rope*!'

'Why's she gonna come down on a bungee rope?'

'Cos she's sick of the goddam STAIRS that's why!'

There are four of these hotels in the eastern half of the road, the Arden, the Urquhart, the Kensington and Table Mountain. Most of the day the young travellers lounge around; early evening they start getting ready; they came around the world for nights in the city. We were turning into the main road when the blond traveller from the train passed us inside on the left, pausing to look through the kebab house window at the cone of meat. 'Three times is enemy action, Mr Bond!' The line came readily to mind.

But it's stranger than that. The coming from afar, the coming nearer; the being here. It is like –

'What else do we need?' Louise wondered. 'Can you think?' She was bending to get a tin of tuna. Her knickers were red. She could have had an eye tattooed at the base of her spine to catch anyone looking at them.

'Nothing.'

'Are you sure?'

It's like seeing rain at a distance, over fields or sea. Those grey cones, over there, east side of the bay, see them swagging? That's rain that is. And now, here – marvellous! – the same rain soaking us, darkening the sand. We actually saw it coming. – Is it like that?

When we left the shop, he was walking away from us carrying his kebab in a parcel like a novice father, so carefully that we overtook him at the corner of our road. The smokers from the steps of the Arden were now up on the balcony whooping. As we passed, the tubby guy nodded.

***

Late in May, Louise asked if we could put up her friend on Saturday night. It turned out the friend's husband was less straightforward than it had been popular to suppose. I said of course, as Louise ennumerated the stages of sexual dissimulation on the fingers of her left hand with the index finger of her right, tup tup tup, looking in my face for indignation. Certainly, it was a tale of wickedness; certainly; a straightforward tale of wickedness, that's what it was.

Anyway, Louise said, now from another room, Georgie'd be here about six o'clock Saturday. First she was going to see a psychologist; then she would drive up. She could sleep in the other bedroom. That would be all right wouldn't it? It would.

She arrived just before seven o'clock, having enjoyed herself with the psychologist and then got caught up in the Whitsun traffic. She looked very bright for a woman in crisis, as if she'd been walking a dog on the beach and become excited by the game of stick-throwing. With my permission, she and Louise seceded to the other bedroom and shut the door. I stood at the window and watched the street. Their voices came through the wall as if I were a trapped miner and they were having a break from knocking their way through to me. Then they would murmur, and I was abandoned. I couldn't move from where I was. They murmured on. After two days, I'd have to drink my own piss. In the twilight, the crossbeam of the kids' swing above the privet hedge of the residents' garden had the appearance of a gibbet. The red sign of Hotel Arden flicked on. The door behind me opened and Georgie and my wife were waiting.

We went along to a new Indian restaurant on the main road. Figures were passing in and out of the balcony of the Arden, laughing and calling others to come out and join them; a couple of dark figures on the street below were called up too. Six or twelve thousand miles they'd come. I wondered how many could fit on it before it collapsed. If you were too old, the whole lot'd come down.

Chettinad Junction was a large place; we were given a concealed table in its western transept. When we'd settled, Georgie told me her troubles, listening eagerly to my responses, while Louise nodded and translated some of my philosophical remarks. There was a lull. The main courses appeared. I didn't want to say too much more: talking about things in particular gives me a parochial feeling, particularly interesting things. The noise of words drives them away. Thinking's better; thinking is quiet.

'Bet you haven't read *Corinth*, Mark!' Georgie glimmered at me.

'He won't read books like that,' Louise chaffed me loyally. She was feeding herself from a noodle bowl the size of a medium lampshade. The noodles steamed and glistened as she sorted them from their yellow broth.

'I've seen it in the shops,' I said. Stacked in pale woody-brown pilasters. The cover of the book, it's the colour of millions of living rooms. Louise looked across, Georgie sideways, at me. They wanted my scornful opinion as sauce to their meal. I couldn't give it. 'You have read it, Georgie?' She had golden powder on her face: Louise must have given it her to cheer her up. She'd left some of her meat.

'I've read it twice.'

'Have you?'

'Yes. I'm ashamed to tell you!' She laughed. She wasn't very ashamed. On the other hand, maybe she lived and read in shame, with her glimmering face. A smell of grapefruit cologne rose from her, more spirituous than the hosts of spices on the air. Single-handed it fought them and died.

'But it's got an interesting theory,' Georgie said. Louise sat patiently, knowing how I liked to hear theories. No noodles were left in her lamspshade. 'The main character's a librarian.'

'Ah.'

'Not an ordinary librarian.' Georgie gave me a chastening look. 'He's won all these research prizes. Don't make that face, Marcus, or I won't tell you!'

'I'm sorry.'

'Anyway he goes to Corinth to do research.'

'What into?'

'The fall of the Greek Empire. Ssh a minute. Anyway, he's in a bar one night sipping an ouzo –'

'Are they all smashing plates in the backgound?'

'No, darling. This is quite a literary bar. Then the barman says to him, "Excuse me, sir. A lady asked me to give you this." It's a note. Richard – that's the librarian: Richard York – Richard asks him when, and the barman says just now. "She was just here now, sir." Which is a mystery because Richard didn't notice anyone. No one had been within his *purview*.' Georgie paused for me to enjoy her word. 'So he opens the note. The lady says she's seen him in the Library of Periander this morning; and yesterday afternoon during the thunder storm. The paper she's written the note on, it's thick in his hands: like parchment – why are you laughing?'

'I'm not!' I protested. Louise kicked me under the table.

'Richard agrees to meet her and they go for dinner. He meets her in a grove beside the bar. She's blonde. She's a sort of ageless beauty. Like Catherine Deneuve.'

'Mark likes Catherine Deneuve,' Louise said maternally. 'Don't you?'

'Yes.'

'Richard's wife's recently left him because of his career. She's left him for a banker. He's very wary of jeopardizing another woman's happiness.'

In his shirt of burnt-orange, the waiter lowered his head to ask if it had been fine for us. Georgie went on. The woman's name was Leda. She exerted a hypnotic effect on Richard: after the brandies, he found he was walking in the rain with her. Then he found he was in the foyer of her hotel, where he said goodbye, remembering he had an appointment with a curator at 8:45 the following morning. The next evening, he rang her at her hotel (as promised) to invite her for dinner. They arranged to meet in the bar at his hotel. He went down to sip a beer – being thirsty from an afternoon among dust and archives – and wait for her. He was startled to find that Leda was there already, her hotel being the other side of town. That night they made love. Richard felt that Leda made love like a mountain climber.

'What are you looking at?' Louise asked me.

'Just someone over there.' At the back of the restaurant, where the burnt-orange wall was painted with a tiger in a cage on tiny green wheels, back straight, head high, he sat in uneasy dominance by two friends.

'Is it the one who was on the train?'

'Yes.' How did she know? When did he come in? 'D'you remember him then?'

'Yes!' Louise said brightly.

'He was on the tube as well.'

'I know he was.'

'And he passed us – when we went to the shop.'

'Yes.'

I was amazed, by her, by the two of us. We'd never discussed him. Not once. I said no more about it. I wondered if he spoke English, to sit over his friends with such glum superiority. We paid the bill and left. Outside it was raining.

'I've got it here, Marcus.' Georgie was taking a book from her weekend bag. 'Hold on,' I said. 'I'm going to have a drink. Would you like one?' I had a brandy, Georgie a glass of port, then we skimmed through *Corinth* for specimens while Louise made Georgie's bed.

'Look at this: *He watched her like a man who has been woken too quickly.* Ha ha ha!'

'It is so rubbishly written!' Georgie laughed.

'Ha! This: *She searched his face as if it were an unknown garden.*' We roared cleverly.

'It's quite an ingenious idea though, the plot idea,' Georgie reminded me.

'Oh yes. So what happens?'

'Well after Leda's slept with him, she starts telling him about her life. Bit by bit. He has to keep sleeping with her to find out the whole thing.'

'Why does he want to?'

'To what?'

'Find out the whole thing?'

Georgie licked her upper lip slightly. The tip of her tongue was swarthy with port. I heard Louise whack a pillow. 'Because she's extraordinary. She's actually a middle spirit.'

'Hey?'

'Now you're interested.'

'How do you know?'

'I can tell. You like things like that.' She held her little glass by the bottom of the stem to drink. 'The Renaissance philosophers were interested in them.'

'In what?'

'Middle spirits. They're in between God and the angels, and humans.'

'Where do they live?' I asked humorously.

'In the upper air. And the clouds. They can move really fast. And they live about two thousand years. Zeus was one. And Apollo. And Helen of Troy. Now don't interrupt. They can do all sorts of things. Fly round the earth for example. But when they die, that's the end.'

'In what sense?'

'They don't go to heaven. It's *finito*.'

'What are you two on about?' Louise had come in.

'Middle spirits.'

'But if they marry a mortal man, they get an immortal soul. That's why Leda is after Richard.' Georgie looked down her nose.

'So what happens?'

'Why don't you read it, Marcus?'

'Yes,' Louise said in sorority.

'I don't fancy it.'

'But you want to know more about it!'

'No I don't. Not that much.' I really was indifferent. Georgie raised her glass at me.

***

When did people stop believing in these things? From other sources than *Corinth* (which was now believed by seventeen or eighteen million people in six different languages), I amassed some information about middle spirits. Ariel was a middle spirit. Mephistopheles too, apparently. And the fairies and nymphs. They could come through keyholes. Paracelsus believed in them, Shakespeare did, Pope too. The belief then faded. Unlike God, they didn't stay too long. They certainly had decorum, your middle spirits; which was why they were now welcome back. If only they hadn't all died. It was sad to think this. It was desolatingly sad; that they'd had their two thousand years and gone.

Unless there were one or two remaining who'd started about 10AD. They'd still have a chance. But they'd be worried; they'd be in their very last years; they'd be looking for – damn it! I was starting to believe all this myself; like seventeen or eighteen million readers of the book I scoffed at. Except that *I* had my own sources.

As the summer went on, I became interested in trying to spot them. The traits I was looking out for were speed of travel, and eagerness for sex (with a potential husband, or wife). I didn't notice any of the former; though of course, they wouldn't want to advertise it in case they alarmed mortals; no doubt they kept away from the aircraft routes. *How quickly did you get here?* was a question constantly on my mind as I observed the people around me. The other trait posed its own problems of detection. Assuming everyone was eager, though not conspicuously – at least not in my area – how did you sift a spirit's desire from the mortals'? I became quiet and watchful. I would sniff a spirit out. There was one hard by us: I knew it.

Underground at Victoria, on the curving platform of the westbound District Line, I was watching the thick sparks of an eastbound train when the blond traveller slotted in. He was listening to a stocky Kiwi with cropped ginger hair who was expostulating about Britain and looking up for approval; which was granted perhaps once with a nod. I found myself on an empty platform, oblivious of my train.

'It will come,' I said to myself, 'it must come.' At the window, I was looking up the road in the twilight. Behind me Louise hovered, wanting to show me the new things she'd bought.

'You keep not saying anything these days,' she complained. 'Is anything wrong, darling?'

'I'm concentrating.'

'What d'you think of this one?' It was a pale gold camisole trimmed with lace. There he was, leaving the hotel beyond the Arden to look for a wife. 'Well?' Louise came down the room and stood with her hands on her hips between me and the window.

'Ha!' I cried. 'That'll do! That *will* do. Very sexy. And very votive!' She left the room happy, returning to say that Georgie would be coming to stay at the weekend. Better still!

As we try to remember dreams, I tried to induce what lay ahead of us by switching off all thought of it but leaving the door open. Let it come. Keep it dark. Mind you don't startle it! I began to feel hilarious, vague, incontinent.

Saturday afternoon, I was directed to absent myself. I must concentrate on something mundane. In Kensington High Street, I examined trousers. Why does the philosopher say, 'Truth is a trouser word'? I went along to Waterstone's to find out, passing the twin pilasters of *Corinth* and its mulberry successor, *Brother Erebus*, on my way downstairs to the philosophy section. The answer discovered, I ascended to the street and stared at the cricket through the window of Dixons till the sun began to slant from Hammersmith.

It was falling on our road from the west when I returned. From the balcony of Hotel Urquhart rose a din. They were starting early up there. Among the oscillating torsos I saw a blond head and a blonde head and a dark head. Eyes lowered, I carried on home in excitement of shame. They were all up there now, the traveller, Georgie and my wife. It was happening. He would take them. We were mixing with the spirits. *We*? Yes. Somehow it would be passed on to me.

When they came in they were giggling. Damn. Why back so soon?

'Mark's here!' Louise said gladly. 'Guess what, darling? That blond traveller asked us to his party!'

'Ah!' I held both her hands in mine. I couldn't speak. Her eyes – were they flashing more than usual?

'You aren't angry are you, honey? – It's just that Georgie wanted a gin and tonic when she got here and we didn't have any so we went to that stupid pub where all the Australians go. He was in there and he invited everyone – not just us. All the time we were there we felt so *old* we couldn't get away quick enough. It was so embarrassing.'

'Didn't you enjoy it at all?'

'Georgie thought she might get off with him. That's really why we went.'

'Ah!' This was more like it. 'Any luck?'

Looking down her nose, Georgie said, 'No! He had no character. *So* gormless. Wasn't my type at all. You're not angry we went are you, Marcus? It was my fault. Lou only came to please me.'

'No,' I said dolefully. 'Not angry. It's not that. What was the party for?'

'He's going back on Monday. He was just here for the summer.'

'Ah you've got lovely new trousers!' Louise stood back to admire the camel linen strides I'd bought, which now hung on my legs like sackcloth. 'I know what'll cheer you up! Just a minute.'

So she brought me a beaker of cask-strength whisky and the three of us smoked some grass. And when I tell them both what I've been thinking, I'm damned if they don't giggle like nymphs at my preposterous conception.

On A Roll

Tania Hershman

We see no patterns in the tossing of a coin, the rolling of dice, the spin of a roulette wheel, so we call them random…'random'… may be inherent, or it may simply reflect human ignorance.

NewScientist 25 September 2004

Holding them by the heels, I set the sandals down on the cloth. My naked toes twitch and wriggle. The croupier's expression doesn't flicker, as if women place their shoes in front of him during every roulette game.

'Six hundred and forty-five dollars,' I whisper. The croupier, the waitress with the pierced eyebrow, Jim from Texas – they can all see the label, they know what these golden babies are worth.

'Brand new. I have the receipt. Six hundred and forty-five,' I say again, feeling braver. This is the way it is meant to be. After all I've been through, right here is where everything is supposed to turn around.

'Mind the heels on the baize, ma'am,' says the croupier. He counts out my chips, pushes them over, and, even though I know what he is about to do, I hold my breath as he picks up my sandals and places them out of arm's reach.

I count my chips: four blood-red hundreds, four night-blue fifties, four bile-yellow tens and a pitch-black five. Four plus four is eight, eight plus eight is sixteen, sixteen plus sixteen is thirty-two, chants a voice in my head. My toes grip the legs of the high chair, my hands shake and I feel dizzy. What the hell have I just done?

But there is also something reassuring about all of this. It is word perfect. Everyone is saying their lines exactly as it was in my dream. They are playing their part so I am playing mine.

Las Vegas was a business trip. The company sent me to meet a client, some old bloke with a plastics factory churning out casino chips. I was there to walk him through the new laser slicer. But mainly I was there, said my boss, because this guy only liked to work with women. Normally the feminist in me would spike up and refuse, but I'd never been to Las Vegas – never been to America at all – so I just saluted and said,

'Yes sir, where's my plane ticket?'

His secretary sorted out a stopover in New York, six hours. That was all I needed.

It was a night flight. I sleep well on planes and I was exhausted, I hadn't had an uninterrupted night since the accident, so I nodded off even before we'd left the ground. I don't know how long I was out for. I woke up suddenly, confused, still inside the surreal dream I'd been having. I don't generally remember dreams, but this one insisted on replaying itself over and over again in my brain, as sharp as a Technicolour film: I am sitting at a roulette table next to Jim from Austin. A croupier with enormous eyebrows spins the wheel, and the waitress, who is heavily made up and has a tongue stud, brings me a Cosmopolitan cocktail. I'm wearing my favourite green dress. On my feet are the new shoes I'm planning to buy in New York, shoes to which I've attached, like a shopping list, all my hopes for a new life. I sit there in my green dress and my gleaming sandals, and I slowly gamble away all my money.

It was like no other dream I'd ever had. It didn't cut randomly from one location to another, people didn't appear out of thin air or have two heads, I didn't sprout wings and fly. Even when I took off my sandals and laid them on the roulette table, it somehow felt real. I sat there on the plane replaying it in my head, something in me wanting to cry like a baby.

I came out of JFK, my head buzzing, and found a taxi.

'Bergdorf Goodman's, please,' I said to the driver, and stared out of the window at the city I'd only seen in films, but my mind was elsewhere.

'Happy shopping, ma'am,' said the taxi driver as I shoved a handful of green money at him, hoping it was the right amount. I nodded, dazed and rather unsure of where I was, but standing there on the pavement, I stared up at the department store logo and a switch inside me clicked. I had a mission. I headed straight in and up to the shoe department, trailing my wheelie case behind me.

There they were.

I asked for my size and whispered to the butterflies in my stomach. Slipping the straps over my ankle, the little Romanesque coins gently knocking into one another, I had to remind myself to breathe. My feet, always ignored in their ugly leather clodhoppers, were suddenly elegant, pale and long. They were someone else's feet, not the feet of a thirty-two-year-old, jet-lagged widow in overlarge jeans and a baggy jumper. They were beautiful feet.

I could have picked a glitzier style with rhinestones, or something plainer and more sophisticated, but when I saw this style online, I fell in love. It was the coins. The coins reminded me of a London museum we'd visited when I was little. I'd dashed past the remnants of perfume jars and animal skins, but stopped short at the case with ancient money. People hundreds and thousands of years ago had used these bent bits of metal to go shopping, like the ten-pence pieces I handed over for ice cream? No, couldn't be. But looking back on it, I believe that what I found most strange was that all these lives had gone on before I was born. Until that moment, I thought the world began and ended with me.

I gave the sandals to the assistant, handed over the cash, and went to catch my next flight.

The hotel room in Las Vegas was bigger than my flat: two double beds, huge windows overlooking the strip from ten floors up, and a very well-stocked minibar. I had time to change my clothes and have a restoratative cup of tea before heading off to my meeting. It went well, he seemed to like me, touching my arm every few minutes as only an aged flirt can get away with, and promised he'd upgrade all their machines by the end of the year. I refused his entreaties to have dinner with him – far beyond the call of duty – and rushed back to the hotel, roulette wheels spinning in my mind.

Sliding my card into the slot, I opened the door, and the ringing silence hit me like lead. I stood frozen in the doorway, wondering why no one was waiting for me, and a fit of hysteria rose inside me like acid. But something stronger forced it down and I took hold of myself. I had something more important to do.

Taking the green silk dress off its hanger, I slid into it and it wrapped itself around me. When I opened the Bergdorf shoebox and saw my heavenly sandals, I felt the need to give thanks. I'm not a praying person. I hadn't prayed in the hospital, there were no words I could think of. All I could do was bawl my eyes out, hoping that some god somewhere would know what I wanted. Maybe I should have tried harder.

I closed my eyes for a minute, and then lifted out the right sandal, tiny coins jangling.

My dream hadn't specified which casino so I went to the nearest, a tacky imitation Greek temple, complete with white pillars and nude statues. I stood in the entrance, high on my heels and dizzy with it all.

With two hundred dollars worth of chips, I looked around for the roulette tables. Crossing the room, the nearest table came into focus – and there they were. A croupier with bushy eyebrows was collecting chips from a balding man sitting with a glass of whisky. The world swam in front of my eyes, and something whispered in my chest, but I didn't stop. Someone was pulling my strings and I let them lead me.

I sat down to the croupier's left, opposite the man who would soon be telling me the story of his three marriages.

'Can I get you a drink, miss?'

I jumped. Thick kohl eyeliner, red lipstick, short dark hair.

'A Cosmopolitan,' I said, the words sounding like a tape recording of my voice playing through my vocal chords. The waitress nodded.

'Are you in, ma'am?' said the croupier.

'Yes,' I said. 'I'm in.'

'You're not from around here, are you?' said the balding man, leaning towards me.

'How can you tell?' I said and smiled. It felt strangely comforting to be inside an experience I had already had, like sinking down into a well-worn couch.

It took me an hour to double my money and then lose it all. I didn't remember what numbers I'd rolled in the dream, so I picked red and black at whim, high and low. I trusted I was doing what I was supposed to.

Jim was down a thousand dollars.

'I just can't hold back,' he sighed. 'Marie's on the machines, she can stay over there for hours, and I just like to watch the pretty little numbers going round.'

I stared at the place where my chips had been.

'Out?' asked the croupier, turning away as if he already knew the answer.

I could have stopped. I could have walked away with nothing but an hour's fun for two hundred dollars. I could have sliced through the strings that had my hands dancing and my tongue moving, and gone back to the hotel and straight to bed. The thought swirled around my mind, but it was no good. I knew what I was going to do. I reached down to undo the strap on my right shoe.

The croupier stands statue-like, my beautiful sandals by his right hand, waiting.

'Well, girl, you gonna do it, blow the lot?' grins Jim. He drains his fifth scotch, watching me.

The waitress whistles softly.

'Honey, I'm not supposed to interfere, but those little darlings, you don't want to just…I mean, you can't…'

I barely hear them. I've gone too far now to stop. I'm inside this thing, and have abdicated control. I take hold of the pile of plastic discs with both hands and push them away from me onto red thirty-two. Thirty-two. That, the dream was very specific about. Thirty-two are the years of my life, I think as I lift my fingers from the chips, and what do I have to show for them? A husband gone, buried before he had a chance to get old, before we could really begin to fit inside one another. I never imagined it would all be over like that. I thought we had all the time in the world, but all we had was an instant.

From almost our first date, Glen talked about having children. He never knew about the one he almost had. I hadn't told him when I found out: we had only just got engaged, we were barely beginning our life together. Now I'm alone, left with nothing of my husband but a wardrobe of T-shirts and jeans and his favourite boots.

I look away from the pile of plastic exchanged for a pair of angel shoes that could have been made for my feet. Folding my hands in my lap, as the dream's stage directions specified, I say: 'Roll,' and the ball begins its journey. Fast at first, it circles the numbers, bumping and jumping from one to another, my eyes can't keep up with its dance. Then it begins to tire, moving around the wheel more lazily, looking for its place. Slower and slower it winds, over ones and twenties, fives and fifteens, and then in to thirty-two it sinks as if it has come home.

And then out.

I lose.

I lose six hundred and forty-five dollars, and I lose my shoes.

The croupier finally shows some emotion. He looks at me, raises his eyebrows and blinks.

'I'm sorry, ma'am,' he says. He gathers the chips to him, and then he slides my sandals into a drawer under the table.

The waitress puts her arm around my shoulder, the Texan offers me a handkerchief. They expect me to cry, to beg and plead with the croupier, to claim that this is unfair, that betting a pair of shoes must surely be against the rules, to threaten to take it to the management.

Instead I stand up.

'Thank you,' I say to the croupier. He nods. Jim winks, wishes me luck.

The waitress, bemused, picks up her tray and takes away my cocktail glass.

Walking towards the doors, my toes sink into the red carpet.

'A good night, ma'am?' says the security guard on the door. Then he sees my feet. His eyes open wide. 'Miss, are you…?'

I don't hear the end of his sentence. I am out in the street barefoot and people are staring at me but I don't care. I am free. I have sacrificed the most perfect things I ever owned. I loved them from the first moment. They were mine for a tiny ripple in the great ocean of time and then they were gone. It is like I have shed my skin and am standing naked and new again. I am Eve in the garden before the snake arrives, and this time I am going to do it right.

Love Of Fate

Anthony Cropper

The little boy was sitting at the end of the table and the man was by his side, helping him with his food. Carefully, the boy placed down his knife and fork.

'Tell me something funny,' he said.

The man thought for a moment then smiled.

'I was out the other night and I asked for a pitcher of water. The waiter brought me a photo of the Atlantic Ocean.'

'I don't understand,' said the boy. 'And how come you get more food than me?'

'I'm bigger than you, as is your mother. We need more fuel inside us. You're bigger than the dog, so you get more fuel than her. It's a size thing.'

The boy cleared his throat and straightened his knife and fork.

'I think I've had enough to eat now. Can we finish the rocket?'

'But you've barely touched it. Just one more mouthful.'

'One more will make my head hurt.'

'Then do you want something else?'

'Did you say you had choc-ices?'

'I did. But not unless you eat some more of that.'

'But choc-ices make my headache go away.'

The man stood up and scraped the remains from one plate to the other. Then, he took the plates and the cutlery through to the kitchen. He filled two glasses with water and returned.

'Your mother said she smelled gas this morning. Did you smell gas?'

'What's gas?'

'It goes underground, for fires, for fuel, for heating. It's in pipes. You can't see it, it's underground.'

'Do trees use gas?'

'No. Trees drink water.'

The man placed the drinks on the table and took his seat.

'And that's underground,' said the boy. 'You told me once there's a table under the ground, and trees have roots that drink water from the table.'

The boy took a sip of his drink.

'Sort of. Yes. Did I tell you that?'

The man glanced out of the window. It was evening. Over the road, above the houses, the sky had turned orange-red.

'Maybe it was a fire, maybe your mother smelt a fire. Sometimes you can smell things from a long long way away.'

The boy sniffed and smiled.

'I can smell Australia.'

'Now that *is* a long way away.'

'It smells like an ostrich.'

'What do I smell like?'

'You smell like, like a truck that's tipping out sand.'

'That's great. You smell of, of…'

'A field with chocolate in.'

'You're too good at this game. I wish I had some of your imagination. You lose a lot when you grow old.'

The boy took a drink of water then gazed around the room.

'I spy with my little eye, something beginning with C.'

'Cloud.'

'No.'

'Car.'

'No.'

'Crayon.'

'No. It's a cement mixer. It went past the window. It's gone now. It's your turn.'

The man stroked his beard and looked back towards the window.

'I spy with my little eye, something beginning with T.'

'Train.'

'Nope.'

'Trampoline.'

'Now where's the trampoline?'

'In the back of that truck over the road.'

'How do you know?'

'There might be.'

'Yes, there might be, but it's not a trampoline.'

'Okay. It's a tree.'

'Yes. That's it. Well done. You're a very clever kid.'

'When will mum be back?'

'She won't be long.'

'Yes. But when will she get here? You said she'd be back soon.'

'She will be.'

'Will she be drunk?'

'No. She'll be fine. Why not do another I spy?'

'I can't think of anything. Can I just sing?'

'Of course you can sing. You're very musical, I can tell.'

'Oh the grand old Duke of York, he had ten thousand ladders, he marched them up to the top of the hill and he marched them down again. And when they were up they were up, and when they were down they were down, and when they were only halfway up, they were neither up nor down.'

The man clapped his hands together and smiled.

'That's fantastic. I like ladders.'

'So do I. You didn't get me a choc-ice.'

'Did I say you could have one?'

'Yes.'

'Ok. I'll get you a choc-ice. Then let's finish that rocket.'

The man stood up again and brushed his hand over the boy's head.

'Are you leaving tonight?' said the boy. 'I saw you packed a suitcase. Are you leaving?'

'I might be. Yes. Probably. I will be. Why don't you sing another song? You've a good voice.'

'I don't know any more songs.'

'Me and your mother. Listen.'

'The first time you came you gave me an aeroplane.'

'Did I? Did I do that?'

'Yes. I hope her next boyfriend is like you.'

The man ruffled the boy's hair.

'He will be. Don't you worry. He will be.'

The Categories Of Ernest Bookbinder

Nathan Ramsden

1. *A Greeting*

Ernest was born in the suburbs. His parents were middle class and lacked aspiration: they owned a semi-detached house with a larch in the front garden and a row of gangly sweet peas at the back. A line of rectangular flagstones led from the patio to a vegetable patch, behind which, partly screened by shrubbery, lay a small pond. Ernest's father, an engineer, had always wanted a pond. He had collected frog spawn as a child, in jam jars stolen from his mother's pantry. He sometimes put them back in there to see what would happen. His mother had not enjoyed the discovery of putrid jelly nestling between the biscuits and condensed milk. His pond was his solace; he would watch boatmen and an occasional newt while he dug over the potatoes. Ernest's mother gave birth at home because she did not like hospitals. Her husband had faith in technology and did not share her distrust of those who wielded it. 'All my family have died in the care of doctors,' she said, neglecting to add she was too embarrassed to be strapped into unflattering stirrups, and feared she would be inappropriately spied upon by medical students whose experience of pudenda was limited to the diagrammatic. The baby was delivered by a cousin.

Ernest was a slight child and urinated an extravagant arc upon his entry into the world. It was his first, and for many years only, transgression.

2. *On Youth*

Ernest grew up looking out of windows. The one in his bedroom provided a view over the back garden. It pleased him, though at the time he did not know why. Fences drew borders on left and right between their garden and those of the neighbours; at the rear was a hedge of bushy leylandii which had grown tall. Over it peeped the mottled clay roof-tiles of houses on the next street. Ernest liked to count the chimneys. There were twenty-seven. He also liked the vegetable patch, though not as much as the patio; he developed a suspicion of the pond.

Of the other windows in the house, Ernest most often sat by the one in the living room, scanning the street as if awaiting someone. His mother was perplexed. 'Play with your toys,' she would say. Ernest had a large and varied collection of die-cast cars and trucks. His favourite game was to set them in a grid across the carpet. Once, his mother came along with the vacuum cleaner and made him heap them on his lap in a chair. Ten minutes later she was back to polish the ornaments. The cars had been returned to their original positions.

The master bedroom played to Ernest's nascent sense of mystery. He longed to enter his parents' private domain and indulge in a new panorama; more, he yearned to throw open their wardrobe and see his father's ties swinging like gamebirds on the rack. His father caught him one day squinting beneath the door. He was going to clip Ernest's ear but was slayed by a look of such sorrow he bent and kissed the boy instead.

The glass in the bathroom overlooked the neighbour's drive but was heavily frosted and passed only slabs of colour. Ernest was ten before he could reach the handle and was unimpressed by the vista. To compensate, he tipped his box of cars onto the floor. After twenty seconds of staring at them unmoved, he realised he had outgrown both his hobbies. The disappointment never left him.

3. *An Education*

Being neither very bright nor very dull, Ernest passed through school unremarkably, though the rougher sort mistrusted him for his lack of sport and indifference to girls. He harboured no desire for either; his parents abandoned attempts to engage him with both.

Unpopularity came as naturally to him as mediocrity. Tenth in an egg-decorating competition one Easter he stepped round a lonely corner of the schoolyard to be confronted with a phalanx of other, disgruntled, losers. A dozen arms were raised; a dozen old eggs were thrown. Ernest calmly walked back into school, where the caretaker helped clean him up and gave him a boiled sweet. The stink followed Ernest for a week; even teachers spurned him. He bore the ignominy with grace.

In the evenings he stayed mostly around the house and was a help to his mother. On his fourteenth birthday his parents bought him a bicycle. Ernest helped bake his own cake. His father choked to death on the icing. Ernest inherited his ties.

4. *On Work*

His mother knew the butcher. She got him a job as assistant. On his first day the butcher took him into a cool room at the back and presented Ernest with the strung carcass of a sheep and an array of knives. The butcher grinned. It was this, as much as the disembowelling, that sent Ernest down the high street in mortal panic.

It transpired the post office required a clerk. Ernest applied in his most rigidly dependable handwriting and was appointed within the week. Being a clerk suited him; a propensity for order allowed him to flourish, as much as is possible for a post office clerk. Ernest's filing earned him a reputation. It outgrew him when it was discovered he had not only perfected the regulation methods but improved upon them secretly. No one could make sense of it; Ernest was let go for insubordination.

5. *On Sex*

After what seemed a polite and proper time, Ernest's mother allowed him to appear happy again in public. It was decided he should improve his standing through lofty social circles; she took him along to church meetings. Ernest did not feel able to relax under the starry, benevolent gaze of two dozen Ladies but became popular. One young member, a girl not much older than Ernest, took a particular liking to him and after morning service coyly suggested it would be a shame to waste such a beautiful day indoors. Ernest agreed, equally coyly, and they strolled down to the park with proud and jealous eyes upon their backs. They hardly spoke. 'What's your name?' she said. 'Ernest,' said Ernest. 'I'm Clarissa,' said Clarissa. Later, Ernest could name two plants and Clarissa was impressed. Clarissa made a daisy chain because it was spring. Mostly, the afternoon passed quietly under the shade of a tree. Ernest had a few coins his mother had given him. He used them to buy fish and chips which they ate together sauntering back. Somewhere between the working men's club and the gasworks, Clarissa took his hand and pushed it up her skirt so his palm lay flat on the front of her pants. Ernest politely left it there as she moved around. She grew hot and damp; Ernest removed himself, thanked her for a lovely time, and ran home. His mother heard the door slam. Ernest spent twenty minutes in the bathroom.

Ernest enjoyed living with his mother. It never occurred to either of them he should attempt independence. She suggested to him he learn to drive. His father would have taught him, but now that was impossible she offered to pay for lessons. Ernest lacked interest but did not complain. The lessons continued for some weeks but he made little progress. His instructor, a fat ex-policeman with a neatly trimmed beard, was helpful and encouraging. One day Ernest stalled amid a crossroads. He felt a warm, pudgy hand come to rest on his thigh. Ernest drove perfectly all the way home with the instructor's fingers nestled next to his crotch, took his leave and cancelled the lessons. When challenged by his mother, Ernest said his bike was enough.

6. *Concerning the Chief Systems*

Success appeared to Ernest in the form of a library. He liked to visit and borrowed regularly. A poster in the window advertised a vacancy and when Ernest had been given the job the staff joked they had lost the one thing that kept them in business. Modestly, Ernest laughed.

He took to wearing his father's too-big suits for work. 'I need to look smart,' he told his mother. 'Dad always looked smart.' 'He did,' said his mother. 'He filled them.' Ernest did not mind. He was happy to bring something of his father back to life.

The head librarian was a glowering man, a little shorter than Ernest but bristling. 'A library is like an army,' he said. 'Efficient and smart. There are ways of doing things.' Ernest remembered the post office.

Things went well. Ernest developed an admirable capacity for recollecting the location of almost every book in the catalogue. There were two competing systems: a musty old microfiche with squealing gears, and a nearly modern computer, the daisywheel printer of which battered headaches into many a head as it rattled and thundered out its faded copy. Ernest was faster than both. Unsuspecting members of the curious public would inquire as to the existence of something recherché and off he would lope, leaving behind his fellow staff in the green basilisk's gaze of the monitor.

7. *Paradise Lost*

Ernest's fame spread throughout the borrowing populace. Performance was expected of him. Library membership was up as people came to demand obscurities. 'Admiral's *Tectonics*,' they would say, 'the rare brown-paper 1942 edition,' or '*Ways to Win at Sumo Wrestling*,' or 'Have you got the one with the green cover? I think it's about bats. Or engines. It's this big.' This last demand elicited something strange from Ernest: a gargling, derisive laugh. The startled customer left piqued; astonished staff began to murmur. They could not remember the last time a sound like that had been heard in the library. Only when its echo had been swallowed wholly did anyone feel able to continue. Ernest left the counter, muttering.

Ernest's efficiency slipped. Constant demand seemed to have bettered him. Everyone noticed the descent into sluggish incompetence. Customers began to complain, sometimes loudly. 'I have come *X* far for nothing,' they would say. Ernest viewed them with contempt. He would deliberately avoid fulfilling requests, vanishing into the depths of the reserve shelves to nibble on biscuits. Discontent spread among the staff. They knew something was afoot, but not precisely what. Several of Ernest's more senior colleagues started picking on him slyly in unobserved moments. They treated him like a child and gave him simple orders in hectoring tones. When Ernest failed to comply, and often when he did, they became aggressive. 'Upstart,' they called him, and 'whippersnapper'. Never before had it occurred to Ernest that a library could be a dangerous place.

8. *Free Will and Determinism*, or *On Liberty*

Ernest found an increasing number of excuses to be alone in the dark, stuffy storage bays away from the counter. He still knew where everything was; the shelves there were regimentally kept, not at all like the jumble sale the public area resembled. After one particularly bitter embarrassment he strode in with a stack of returned books and distributed them at random. The act awoke in him a trembling pleasure. He treated himself to a biscuit.

The head librarian took to following Ernest round as much as routine allowed. His disappearances had been noted. Ernest's trivial revenge necessarily spread to other, less visible, activities: failing to process orders on time; not renewing books, thereby landing innocent borrowers with unwarranted fines; reinserting deleted items into the shelves but not the system, throwing the place into chaos as the discrepancies mounted and people attempted to borrow books that did not officially exist; and, as opportunity permitted, he continued his disordering of the bowels of the building, leaving no obvious sign of his passing but a dainty trail of crumbs.

If anyone had stopped Ernest, and asked him why he had changed, he would have shrugged. He did not know how to explain change.

9. *When Words Collide*

Ernest's behaviour at the library became intolerable once it was discovered. While locking doors the caretaker saw him tear pages from one book and insert them into another. The head librarian was not impressed. 'I wouldn't have said anything,' the caretaker told him, 'but it's Health and Safety. There shouldn't be nobody about by that time. There might be a fire.' It was an observation that tarnished Ernest's fondness for caretakers.

The head librarian approached Ernest about the matter of his employment. 'About the matter of your employment,' he said. 'You no longer have any. It is not required that you attend the library tomorrow.' Ernest was sallow and had crumbs on his chin. 'You respond badly to pressure,' said the head librarian. Ernest's reply is not recorded, but the head librarian bore ever thenceforth a look of surprise. That night Ernest drank a bottle of whisky and rode his bicycle into the pond. It had grown thick with slime. He woke the next morning shivering wet and bedecked in a tangle of weeds. He chose not to remove them.

10. *La Bête Humaine*

Soon after a policeman arrived. No one had seen Ernest for days; his mother had uncharacteristically missed church, and not just once. The Ladies had organised an exploration. As the bobby rapped on the door, they huddled at the gate and peered intently as though their combined efforts would penetrate it.

Time passed. People gathered.

A second policeman was sent for. Together they broke down the door. Five minutes later one emerged and cordoned off the premises. Ernest was escorted to a car and driven away. Those who caught a glimpse of him did not recognise what they saw. It was said he had become transparent, sprouted mould, grown scaly.

11. *How Our Mind Tangles Itself Up*

The policemen had found Ernest cross-legged on his bed staring and mumbling out of the window. He was counting chimneys. They made notes on what they found:

· Forks, bicycle parts, hair products, various household items & such arranged neatly in rows across all the floors. Books alphabetical, furniture by size, &c. Ties in a way we cannot fathom.

· Labels everywhere, all numbered & some with letters.

· Lists made of all the above, cross-referenced.

· Mother, deceased.

She was given A Good Christian Burial, and the Ladies mourned; Ernest did not attend. The idea had been deemed a bad one by the authorities.

12. *Paradise Regained*

Ernest was taken to a secure institution where, the doctors said, he would be safe and cared for. He was placed in Room 143, and had regular exercise.

It would have pleased him, had he the faculty for it, to know there was a place for him in the world.

In Attendance

Paula Rawsthorne

I never really planned to bury myself alive, but now that I have, it somehow feels right. I suppose it wasn't such a big step. No one seems to have noticed anyway.

I realise that this job is a godsend but since becoming the attendant for the Ladies public convenience under City Square, I've become invisible. There's always customers, caught short, desperate (well they'd have to be to come down here) but I can go days without anyone seeing me. I can be polishing the mottled mirror that they're preening themselves in and they just look right through me. I could be doing a naked sword dance, using crossed mops and still they wouldn't flicker. I know in your fifties you can't expect to be turning heads but it's not that; they're worried you see; worried that if they make eye contact they'll have to tip me. What do they think I am; a beggar, some kind of gypsy? This is a council run facility. I get a wage. I'm a trained cleansing technician.

It suits me fine. I've never been one for small talk. Marty was the talker in our house. He could talk for hours. What he didn't know about current affairs wasn't worth knowing. He used to get so worked up about the state of this country – believed it had gone to the dogs ever since Mrs Thatcher was betrayed by her own. He'd say, 'Now there's a woman with balls.' He'd lost both of his by the end but it still didn't save him.

Apparently they sent letters but anything official looking I tended to put unopened in a drawer. Always think that if it's that important they'd send someone around. Well they did eventually; a very presentable young man from the housing office talking about rent arrears and payment plans. I had no idea I was so behind. Truth is Marty dealt with all that side of things. We had a nice little system. I'd hand over my wages from the cleaning jobs and he'd pass me back the housekeeping. I didn't need any cheque book or cash card; if I wanted a little extra I'd just ask. It wasn't a problem most of the time.

Anyway I did the right thing. What did I need with a two-bedroom house? Rattling around, with all those shadows jumping out at me. He really was very nice that young man; asking me was I sure and where did I have to go? Told him that I was going to live with Rachel, my daughter – she insisted, wouldn't take no for an answer. He said, 'That's nice, you don't get that much nowadays.'

I gave the lot away, just kept the essentials. It's been such an eye-opener how little you really need. I phoned some charity in the Yellow Pages and they came with a big van and took everything – well it was easier than trying to sell the stuff. I saw a couple of curtains twitching but no one enquired; why would they? I was never a great mixer. Marty would say, 'Why do you need friends when you've got me?' He was such a looker when we first met. He could have had any girl he wanted but he chose me. Said I wasn't pushy like the others, they all had too much to say for themselves. He said that he could tell we'd make a great team. My parents thought he was wonderful. They couldn't believe my luck.

I tried my best to get hold of Rachel when her dad died. I even went to see the 'in-laws'. They kept me on the doorstep which was a relief. You could tell by the hallway that the house was filthy and they had the cheek to look at *me* as if *I* were dirt. I knew they wouldn't help. They said, all high and mighty like, if Rachel ever wants to make contact it's her decision and they won't be giving me any information. They wouldn't even show me a photo of Jessica. She's my grandchild too. There's not a day goes by I don't think about her, hoping she looks more like Rachel than him. One of Rachel's friends let it slip; that's the only reason I got to know. She'll be eight now. I wish I knew her birthday though. Every year, around the time, I've sent a card, care of the in-laws. I've never kidded myself that they'd pass them on. Scum – that's what they are. No wonder their son turned out the way he did.

Even on the day of the funeral I hoped she might turn up; maybe seen the notice in the paper; but no. There wasn't a big turnout, just a few of his colleagues from the taxis and a couple of his drinking pals. The vicar was a sharp bloke. He said some lovely things about Marty at the service. Nobody would have guessed that he'd never met him. Marty wasn't the spiritual type. He used to say, 'God and religion are for the feeble-minded,' – I didn't like to disagree. Anyway it won't do him any harm.

I don't get regulars, only the druggies and lunatic bag ladies and I chase *them* out straight away. But there was one young woman, came in a few times; a lovely looking girl, glossy hair, beautiful nails. I gave her change for the Tampax machine once. Then, as she was leaving, she smiled and handed me two of those thick glossy mags. Well I was quite overwhelmed, but my God, what a load of rubbish. Packed full of filth – is nothing out of bounds these days?

If you're not doing it every which way, five times a day, there's something wrong with you. Luckily life was a lot simpler for me. Marty never bothered me much after Rachel was born.

I complained to Pauline about the lighting months ago. She was on one of her flying visits. She always comes in panting, 'Those steps will be the death of me.' I showed her all the strip lights on the blink. Their flickering is enough to send you into a fit and the noise; my God, it's like a swarm of kamikaze bees flying into a live wire. Even after I turn the damn things off I still hear them. But it was the usual story. She says, 'I'll send someone from maintenance, just try whacking the starter with the mop handle for now.'

Tells me that the council haven't got the budget to refurbish, but not to worry. 'It's an important city centre facility and it's not on any closure list.' Next thing I knew she was in the office (well they call it an office but it's more like a store cupboard with windows; somewhere to survey my kingdom from). She starts rifling through the supply cabinet, checking up on me, and that's when she found them. 'Are these all your clothes in here, June? What do you need them for, costume changes?' She really tickled herself. All her chins wobbled with laughter. I just said something about going to the launderette but then she pulled out the blankets. 'And don't tell me you get cold, this place is like a bloody furnace.' At least the heat means she never stays long. Day after day, night after night, long after the rusty hand driers have stopped belching out their stale air, those radiators are still red hot. No one's able to turn them off; beyond their control apparently. So I'm left living in a sauna full of bleach fumes.

It doesn't matter how much I scrub this place, it won't be up for any awards. It'll always have that grubby look. Decades of ingrained dirt that's seeped into the tiles and yellowed the grouting; an ocean of hard water that's eaten into the taps and left trails of green down the sinks and toilet bowls. Apparently they replaced the cubicles in the eighties. Looks like it too; cheap, grey Formica boxes creaking and leaning like a row of drunks. On top of everything it's no good for the handicaps and the baby-changing unit has never been touched. Well you wouldn't chance leaving your pram up top, some yobs would be joyriding in it before your back was turned.

Still I do my best, make sure I get right behind the pedestals and in the corners. But it's the young ones, they always hover and the mess they make, like spraying cats. They ignore my signs – go chucking their sanitary products down the toilets. I don't think half of them can read, they certainly can't spell by the look of the graffiti I scrub off.

I don't know what's gone wrong with young women today. I had a group of girls in just before closing the other evening. They'd obviously been drinking, the bride-to-be tottered over to me in her high heels and L-plates, squints at my badge and says, 'June, were you in that film *Strictly Ballroom*?' Suddenly the gang of them were bent double, cackling. The blushing bride slid down the wall in hysterics, thong on display, boobs escaping from her angel outfit.

People are so ignorant. What do they think I should look like, Mrs Mop? Headscarf and slippers with a fag hanging out of my mouth? I always made sure I looked my best for Marty. He didn't want to come home after a long shift and find me looking like something that the cat's dragged in.

When the whole hair thing happened it was a shock to both of us. I could tell he was repulsed – well what husband wouldn't be? In less than four days every strand had fallen out, and I'm not just talking about my head. The doctor did some tests – said that he couldn't find any 'physiological' cause and had I been experiencing any stress recently. Said he could refer me to a counsellor; kept on at me until I cried. Well I said to him, 'I hope you're not implying that I'm not right in the head?' Then I walked out, my head held high. I haven't been to a doctor's since.

I got it on the NHS: Monroe blonde and piled high. I pencil in Garbo eyebrows, choose my lashes and let my make-up bag do the rest – simple yet glamorous. I tend to leave it all on now, just touch it up in the morning before I open. Truth is, the last time I stripped it off, some jaundiced ghoul was staring back at me; hollow cheeks and dead eyes held up by bags the size of life jackets. Marty will be turning in his grave.

At first I did okay. I'd go up top quite the thing – sometimes even for a stroll in the evenings. But then I started to worry that I might be spotted going back down. I could get into a lot of trouble. I'd be sacked for starters and if the local rag got hold of it they'd twist everything; make me out to be some nutter. So I realised that there wasn't much point going out. It's not like I have places to go or people to meet and I've got tons of cup-a-soups, tea bags and powdered milk. Pauline goes on at me every visit, says I'm wasting away. She keeps bringing me those build-up drinks and asking if everything is all right at home. I said to her once, 'We haven't all got appetites like you, Pauline.' That shut her up.

Me and Rachel were inseparable once. She was never so close to

Marty but then he didn't have the time to spend with her although he always made sure he was around for bath and bedtime. It was their special time together; he used to shoo me away. He was good like that, some fathers don't do a tap. But she was always a mummy's girl, clingy even. She'd get all worked up, want me to do everything. Marty got terribly upset; used to say that she didn't love him. It got so bad I had to bribe her. Promised her all sorts if she didn't make a fuss. Sometimes she'd take the treats and start creating regardless and I'd tell her, 'Rachel, a deal's a deal.' She calmed down eventually. Kids go through funny phases don't they?

It may feel like a catacomb down here but the noise is enough to wake the dead. If it's not the pipes banging and the taps dripping it's *them*. They know I close at seven o'clock, but night after night I hear them stumbling down those steps, all tanked up, cursing and kicking the door. More often than not they just drop their knickers and do it in the doorway. Animals – the stench in the morning – I shouldn't have to deal with that.

Anyway, I've got the office quite cosy. Big vase of silk flowers, a few photos, though there's no decent ones of Rachel. She was always hiding that beautiful face behind a mop of hair. No matter how I went on at her, she never took pride in her appearance. The folding chair suits me fine. I tend to doze rather than sleep. My mind keeps kicking me awake. It's full of nonsense – always flitting from one ridiculous thought to another; never finishing what it starts. That's why I put up my postcard: 'A view over Buttermere'. Not that I've been there. We had our week in Torremolinos every year without fail. Marty loved it there. Said you wouldn't know you were in Spain.

What I do is get really comfy, blankets padding my chair, cup of tea in hand and that Classic FM on the radio. I put the volume up as loud as I dare until it turns this cave into the Albert Hall. Then I concentrate on that postcard until I swear I'm there, on top of that mountain, leaning against the wind, arms outstretched. The air so crisp that it slices right through me and the view. There's not a cracked tile or bleached loo in sight; just a huge mirror-lake surrounded by a crown of mountains daring me to reach out to them. Then this sobbing starts butting in. But I'm determined not to be distracted and I'm still there, filling my lungs with that priceless air and I'm overwhelmed by the urge to launch myself off that peak and let the wind carry me across the lake, and I feel so alive, so powerful. But that appalling sobbing just won't stop. Instead it gets louder and deeper until it's swamped my view, drowned out my heavenly music. Until all I can feel is my soaking face and snot streaming onto my heaving chest and I sit there exhausted and terrified as all those thoughts come flooding back again. It's always happening but I just can't help looking at that postcard. Marty would be ashamed of me – he couldn't abide emotional women.

Rachel turned into one of those sullen teenagers. I kept hoping that she'd grow out of it, but then she got involved with that JJ – a right waster, piercings everywhere. Worked at a car wash, *a car wash*, I ask you. We kept warning her. We wouldn't have him near the house so she started staying out all night.

Then late one night Marty had just pulled up on the driveway and he jumped him. I heard the commotion and looked out of the window and saw them. JJ had him on the ground, kicking him in the stomach and his privates. His face was all twisted, bawling abuse at Marty about God knows what. Marty all curled up whining like some wounded animal. I opened the window and screamed, 'I've called the police.' He gave him one last almighty kick and ran off.

Marty was in a terrible state. Three broken ribs, horrendous bruising – said his privates looked deformed. I'm convinced that's what set the cancer off. But he wouldn't have the police involved. Said he didn't want Rachel dragged into it all. He was always thinking of her. Well we couldn't let it go on. Marty said to her, 'Rachel it's him or us.' She actually spat in his face. I was shaking. 'Rachel, Rachel apologise to your father at once.' Do you know, she just turned round to me looking like she had a bad taste in her mouth and said, 'You pathetic cow.' Then she left. That was almost nine years ago now. Brainwashed that's what she was. I can't believe they're still together.

Pauline said the council was on a drive to stamp out threats to employees. So she put up a poster: 'Abusive behaviour towards staff will not be tolerated'. Fat lot of good it does. I had this scrawny girl in a while back, ranting and raving at me because she'd put three pounds in the condom dispenser and got nothing out. Nine a.m. this was, so I knew what her game was. I've got the key but I didn't tell her that. Told her to ring the company if she had a complaint. She screamed right in my face, 'You useless bitch.' Next time I spotted her as soon as she came in. She'd been in the cubicle for ages so I guessed what she was doing. I find a lot of their filthy needles. The police are useless, they never bother. So I start banging on the door. Then I have to look over from the next cubicle and there she was slumped over the toilet, vomit everywhere. Well I was furious, really bawled at her. I didn't realise she was dead. They took her out in one of those body-bags. I had to give a short statement. They said that they wouldn't need to bother me again. The policewoman reckoned she was no more than fifteen. What kind of parents would let that happen to their child? Some people shouldn't be allowed to have kids.

It's easy to lose track of time down here; before I knew it I hadn't been out for three whole weeks. Well, I thought, this is ridiculous. So that lunchtime I made myself climb those steps. When I reached the top I was soaked through with sweat. I could feel my heart banging in my head. I stood tall and tried to gather myself but it was no good. The sunlight attacked me and the disgusting smells and sounds turned my stomach and then the people; swarming towards me like an army of ants. Then it started. I couldn't catch my breath, it felt like a giant fist tightening around my chest, and the more I tried to gulp in air the stronger the grip got. I was ripping at my collar, losing control and all I could think was – I'm going to die. And then the real terror took hold as I realised that any second now I was going to have to face Him and He'll know *everything*, everything. And what horrors He will have in store for me. And as I slid to the floor I begged Him to give me more time, more time to prove to Him that I really am sorry.

Next thing I remember was this honey-coated voice saying 'Breathe slowly and deeply – in then out.' She had a paper bag to my mouth, she said she'd done first aid as she shooed the gawping crowd away. She rubbed my shoulders and kept repeating really slowly, 'In then out.' I watched that bag go up and down and I could feel the grip loosening. I felt so relaxed, like a big bar of melting chocolate. But then she started with the questions. Could she take me somewhere to be looked at? Did I have someone to be with? I shouldn't be on my own. I got rid of her eventually – told her I was meeting my husband and when she was out of sight I crawled back down and I haven't been out since. I couldn't tell you how long ago that was, but I *can* tell you one thing for sure; next time I leave this place they'll have to carry me out just like they did that girl. You see when I make a promise I keep it. I've always believed that a deal's a deal.

Side Exit

Daithidh MacEochaidh

Such a time since he'd taken a journey north of the Wash. Everything was different, although he couldn't help think that nothing that mattered had altered at all. It was this presentiment which stung him still, that years didn't matter, no progress had been made. The nation patched and bodged, but nothing really new had been created. It was like the roadworks, where men in fluorescent jackets had been making good, a modern surface smothering the straight line of a Roman road. Hard work. These men had sweated over the bubbling asphalt like slaves laying the stones for the emperor. He'd thought to make a shortcut through some of the old villages that he had frequented, when stationed during his national service.

National service: you mentioned it now and either people didn't know what the term meant or they confused it with Dad's Army, making light of it all. Just before the bend, just by the baggy oak tree, he knew he could have cut a right and avoided the delay taking a track that would link up with the upper road. That he should have done, but he wouldn't take any risks, misled by memories of supposed good times or be waylaid by the present, some new ring road or housing scheme perhaps.

No, the straight road ahead, despite delays, would suffice. Ironic that his son should have ended up a mere thirty miles from where he had been based: that time of revelations and changes that had so altered him. Some dilapidated line of huts, similar to an old airfield that he had passed, had been where he first saw the world differently; his national service giving him an enthusiasm and determination to give a lifetime of service, and not just to one nation alone. Ideas and ideals, he fixed his mind on them even as he made out the dim spike of Lincoln Cathedral, pricking the skyline ahead.

More delays, single lane again, workers sweating at the side of the road. By a coned-off section, a sign stood proud which he found tickled his somewhat peculiar sense of humour:

NO Hat
NO Vest
NO Boots
NO Job!

There was the hint of something militaristic about it, regimented, controlled and disciplined, nothing ambivalent and honestly direct. It was also pathetic. As if, by implication, that a hat, a vest and a pair of boots could guarantee employment – such a simple solution. He'd fought for simple solutions: full employment, the right to work, beating the boom-and-bust machinations of the market – the future. He'd liked to think that there really had been a time when he had fought for the future. It made sense of what he was doing now, even after all this time.

A squat workman, red-faced and sweating, turned his sign and waved him on. Unfit, fat and unhealthy these younger men. He remembered rationing, that in spite of hardship, the country as a whole had never been so well fed. The State could feed, clothe and organise its people properly, if it wanted – the war had proved that.

Yet the shadow of the war had blighted his youth. Later, the crass stupidity of doing national service had stolen time from him, although something had been put back in its stead; a togetherness, a basic consensus and underlying sense of solidarity to those times. And a belief and a commitment, despite differences, that things were going to be different; it was possible to rebuild. He fought and had campaigned for that.

A car streaked by, music blaring, the window down, 'Stupid old wanker.' The engine moved through the gears, gracefully, nothing hurried, forced or anxious. The slowness was measure enough of any latent anxiety. The car picked up speed gradually. The road still lay ahead. It hadn't moved. And, he was no longer in any hurry to get anywhere. In a quarter of an hour, he knew that he would arrive in good time, with some five minutes or so to spare, despite the delays. All of this, he had clearly mapped out and accounted for almost as soon as the meeting had been agreed upon. That had been the hardest and the most unsure movement that had to be made. He had known that this meeting would come.

Planning, something that he had excelled at. Further, ensuring that plans succeeded as designed was something over which he had delighted. At the council, he had been known as a stickler, though never a bosses' man or a jobsworth. The labourer is worth his hire – his motto. He'd given good service, demanded a decent wage for doing his job to the best of his abilities, nothing more. It still smarted that they had offered him redundancy; insulting to somehow suggest that it was in his best interest. He'd stuck it out, retrained at his own expense, night classes, where he had mastered the skills required for using a desktop computer, the sending of electronic mail, and even designing a few simple and straightforward macros. He'd worked his time. No one had carried him. A labourer is worth his hire.

No Hat No Vest No Boots No Job!

There was something to that, sensible and inherently right.

Sign of the chef, nothing wrong with his eyesight. Indicating in good time, he made the turn, parked between a black Mercedes and a marine blue Toyota. Carefully, he removed his glasses, packing them into their case, safely enwrapped. He had these particular glasses seventeen years come September and good as new. Getting out, he noticed a woman in the Mercedes – resigned shake of the head. The car was littered with clothing, spread to dry upon the back seats: pants, bras and things. The woman read a tabloid, obliviously listening to a wireless, playing loud enough for him to hear. None of his business, he had no right to pry, but he took his time, ensuring that the car was properly locked; walking the narrow corridor between the vehicles, just to be sure, taking his time. He never asked of what he wanted to be sure. The question unasked, unanswered, and the woman read on, ignorant of the man stealing past her car, skirting the perimeter, wary as a prison guard dog.

Finally, tutting, he set at a brisk march to the door. His grip was firm on the handle. The door didn't move. He squinted, saw the sign:

He muttered aloud, something about nothing working as it should in this damn country, anymore. The side door opened without incident. He bought a small cup of tea, taking a seat by the door, so as to see or to be seen. No point hiding; no point trekking halfway up the country, then faddling about when it came to the rendezvous. A smile, brittle and somewhat faint, stole across his lips. He had caught himself just in time, his hand snaking out to the sugar set on the table. He still craved his regimental two lumps. In all of their forty years of marriage, Judith had never forgot to sugar his tea, correctly. One sugar is not enough for a strong, British cuppa, while three is far too sweet and often wasteful, an undissolved slush pooled at the bottom. Two is quite a sufficiency. The doctor had said, too much sugar in his urine. Oh well, it could have been worse. At least it explained why he was visiting the toilet so frequently. Harold, a former civil servant in the foreign office, a man who too had given loyal service, one of his keenest allies at the carpet bowls club, well he, Harold Winters, had faired far worse. Half the night going to the toilet and when finally he saw the specialist at the hospital it was too late. Harold Winters, H.E.O. foreign office, had died just before his sixty-seventh birthday through prostate cancer. As if pushed by some Pavlovian impulse, he made his way to the conveniences.

When he returned, he sighed, but not too loudly. His tea removed, half-drunk, and his table taken by two lorry-driver types, full of tattoos, tabloids full of right-wing tosh and dolly-birds' tits, tabs sucked down to the nubbins hung from their lips, scattering ash all over the table. In a curious way, they reminded him of Yanks. He'd resented the Yanks coming over. No morals. They'd chase the orphanage girls most of them not even sixteen. They tried to bribe him and other lads with chocolate or fags to bring out the girls for them. They were so brash – the manners and morals of animals. Yes, he resented the Yanks, resented more that empty platitude so commonly voiced by them or even by the British themselves, that the USA had saved Europe. As if the disaster of Hitler's Eastern Offensive, as if the massive sacrifices of the Soviet Union, had counted for nothing in the Third Reich's collapse. His reveries broken, a young man, tepidly tugging his elbow.

'Excuse me, are you Malcolm?'

'I am Mr Malcolm Taylor.'

'I'm Karl.'

'Yes, good, pleased you've arrived – good journey?'

'Sort of.'

'How do you mean?'

'Roadworks…I say, would you like to take a seat?'

'I was sitting there.' He pointed to the table where the 'lorry-driver' types still slouched. 'I sat there to ensure that we didn't miss each other.'

'Never mind, eh – I've a table by the window.' Karl tried to guide the elder man over to a chair.

'Ablutions, you know.'

'Never mind, must have only just missed you,' said Karl, rather more successfully moving the man to his table. 'Can I get you anything: tea, coffee, soft drink – something to eat perhaps?'

'A cup of tea, please.'

'Just tea?'

'Just the tea shall be sufficient,' said the man. Did he have to repeat himself? Had his son turned out to be some kind of idiot? Or, was this now what passed for good manners: repetitious dithering? He shook his head slightly.

The place wasn't full. Why those drivers hadn't sat down somewhere else and found their own seat he just couldn't fathom. Irritable, he knew he was feeling irritable again. It was bad for his blood pressure or so the doctor had said. But it was galling…Perhaps, it wasn't so annoying, just the long journey, perhaps there were other reasons why he tended to behave so curmudgeonly these days, but reasons didn't help. He felt like going over there and saying his piece, he felt like he could really say something to those slobs.

'There you go, Dad…' Karl placed two cups on the table, slightly spilling the contents of one. He gave his father the full cup and made sure that it was within easy reach. He took his seat and gazed across at this old man, this stranger. He searched, he took in every line and feature, trying to find some point of resemblance, then lowered his eyes down to the cup. 'I have no right to call you dad or father or…'

'No. I haven't been a father to you.' The old man, Mr Malcolm Taylor, looked down. His fingers had a slight tremble to them when they groped out slightly for the cup; the cup shaking as it was raised to the lips.

The son, Karl, looked at the motion, looked at the face again. His social worker had shewn him a picture of Mr Malcolm Taylor. Mr Malcolm Taylor had sent a photograph for Karl when he had been contacted, along with an address and telephone number. Karl had said to Gene, as he waved the photo-booth Polaroid under her nose, how much he looked like his father. Gene hadn't said anything. Her arm, though, had looped around his waist; she had pulled him gently towards her, then rested her head on his shoulder. He'd liked that. Karl wished his wife was here, had been 'allowed' to attend the meeting.

Karl brought his cup of tea to his lips and sipped. There was silence. Even in that place of quick service and fast meals, amidst the clatter of cutlery, the banging of cups, chatter and occasional laughter there was some small silence, polite as unvoiced prayer, taking up room at that table by the window. It hadn't long. The tea was drunk. The older man made no secret of looking at his watch. The younger man bit his fingers, getting in the way of words for a time. But, words, words had to be spoken. Mr Malcolm Taylor had travelled a long way. He, for one, did not want to dally. 'So, Karl, I was contacted. Not that I minded. I had always let it be known that if I was ever needed in this capacity that I was willing to do the necessary. So, young man, don't mind my manner, but I have always been something of a blunt speaker. How may I help?'

A small bit of friable nail came away. Karl chewed. He'd lost those words, those eager words waiting, all queued, they'd melted away, leaving him a slither of a nail to disseminate and pick over. Fighting for time, hoping that his words would come to him, he reached for the pictures. In his head he tried to find that question list he and Gene had made, those practised parcels of speech. Maybe they would come to him after all, as he searched through his jacket for the photographs, but when he found them, when it came to laying them down on the table, the only words that came were the obvious, the perfunctory, words that scarcely counted.

'That's Gene, my wife, well common-law wife that is really, but we're hoping to get married after Christmas, more like Easter, if we can afford it. Meaning to do it for years, somehow we never seemed to get round to it, or couldn't afford it.' He was rambling slightly and knew it. He battled on, the words would come, he knew that if he could just keep talking. 'We'll let you know when...This is the boys, Martin and Joe. Martin is really Gene's son from an earlier marriage, but I've known him since he was two – and his own father never bothers with him...' Karl coloured up, badly. His hands trembled, trembled so that he didn't turn his last photograph over. 'Sorry.'

'Don't have to apologise.' Mr Malcolm Taylor looked surprised. What was there to apologise over?

'Joe though is mine, mine and Gene's, eight next and a right handful already. You know what they are like at that age...I mean, in general, the way youngsters are these days.'

His father sparked at that, thrusting his shoulders back and clearing his throat before delivering his opinion upon the matter. 'Discipline. They are just allowed to roam the streets at all hours of the night. It's not as if they have nowhere to go: parks, roller-parks, youth clubs and the like. But, do you see them there? No, they're too busy tormenting pensioners or getting into drugs or vandalism. I thought if you made the right environment, you made the right man. The houses, the estates, the playing fields and utilities that these youngsters have are –'

'Joe's nothing like that.'

'Do you always interrupt?' said Mr Malcolm Taylor. Karl was stunned. He looked down at the picture of his wife and his sons. There was that other picture too, but he wouldn't look at that just yet, not now.

'I suppose I should say sorry. I forget how rude I sound. But, so far you haven't answered my question. Why this? Why do you want to see me? How can I help?' said Mr Malcolm Taylor, politely.

'I…I want to know why?'

'What, precisely?'

Karl looked up, faced his father, some of his words were there, at last. 'Why did you and your wife give me up for adoption? You were not hard up. You had your own house. Lower middle class, said the social worker. You could have afforded me. Why did you give me up?' said Karl. There was a certain redness to his face. It could have been pain. It could have been anger. Karl might have been ready to blurt it all out.

'You think you have a right to know that? That the secrets between a man and wife concern you? You are someone whom I do not even know, yet you demand to pry into my wife's and mine's deepest secrets.'

The red had gone from Karl's cheeks. This was not how it was supposed to be. This was not how he had imagined meeting his father. Gene, the social worker, they had done a lot of work preparing him for this, but this was not how it should go. Some cold prick giving him grief for wanting…for finally wanting to know why?

'That's exactly what I want. Tell me, since you've come all this way and not here five minutes and eager to leave. Tell me before you go just why you gave me up, when you could have been my father instead.'

'I see that I have hurt you. Never my intention, but merely so as you know the gravity of what you are asking. Worse, you ask this of someone who freely admits that they are somewhat cold; a cold-fish – do people still say that?'

'They say that.'

Brief silence, a slurp of tea. 'My wife and I did not want children. I was indifferent. I blame my upbringing; raised in an orphanage run by the Poor Clares.'

'You were an orphan too!' This again was not how any of this should have been. He began to wonder about his father now, wonder in ways that he had never dreamt. Hopefully, there were some things that were not shared in common.

'Yes, I was raised by nuns. They were disciplined. If not exactly cruel, they were emotionally indifferent, too caught up with their otherworldly mumbo jumbo to bother about this world and its inhabitants. What is it that Marx says, the philosophers have interpreted the world, but the point is to change it – something like that? Well, these nuns didn't even see this world, too busy on their knees looking up trying to find another one. What is it that Marx says, religion is the opium of the people.'

'Stuff what Marx said. What do you have to say, about anything?' said Karl, his voice at first quick and angry, before becoming quieter, softer, as if speaking to himself.

'I'm sorry if I seem to be straying off the point, but, please, try not to interrupt, as I am, quite genuinely, trying to tell you something.' Mr Malcolm Taylor, stopped, coughed dryly and pensively looked down at the table. Perhaps, he too was searching for words, the right thing to say, or, even, just to speak.

'Sorry…go on. It's only that –'

'I know. I can understand. I too have wondered how I came to be adopted. The most credible story that I was given was that a young catholic girl from Roscommon came over here to work, and fell pregnant. She had me, then returned to Ireland – that was it really.' The man absentmindedly reached down for his drink. The cup was empty.

'Would you like another?' said Karl.

'Why not, but please let me get them.' Mr Malcolm Taylor patiently queued, bought two teas and a small cellophane packet containing biscuits that were sold under the name of cookies. Americanisms. It wouldn't be long before the whole world would be speaking some dialect of American English. Why not? They had won. The West had won and the East was no more than some bankrupt cul-de-sac of history. He was thankful that Judith had died before the final collapse. She still hoped, hoped for a better this world, right to the end, never once looked upwards or inwards, fierce in her atheism. What fireworks, what vitriol there would have been had she lived on to see Blair's Britain and his New Labour. The temper. She was so passionate. The boy seemed a bit emotional, perhaps he had inherited that from Judith.

'There you go, Karl,' he said, putting the drink and the cookies on the table by his son. His bones, his old bones, cracked a little as he returned to his seat. For a while they sipped at their teas, then Mr Malcolm Taylor talked, tried to explain more about the decision reached back then.

'As you can see, I am somewhat detached. I do not naturally warm to my fellow man, which is ironic really, as we, that is to say my wife and I, always tried to work towards the good of our fellow man.'

'All the Marx stuff.'

'Very committed Marxists. It wasn't a dirty word back then, or rather to some it was, while to others it was a cry to freedom. Two sergeants opened my eyes when I did my national service. They'd seen what Capitalism had done first hand –'

'The Nazis…surely?' Karl did a strange thing, he blushed, his face was trying to say sorry for interrupting yet again.

'The Nazis did not drop the atom bomb. But let us not get sidetracked, though it does have a bearing on the way your mother, in particular, thought it a crime to bring a child into this world…You want to know why we gave you up. Simply put, your mother never wanted children. You were a rare mistake.'

Karl thought he had flinched. He wanted to have flinched, but he had just sat there as stark words were so spoken.

'Judith did not want to bring life into a world of the atom bomb, the Cold War and human injustice. You were a late slip-up, despite the precautions we took, not that our marriage was particularly passionate. That sort of thing wasn't so important in our day, and, besides, ours was a marriage of ideals and ideas really. Yet come along you did and we did bring life into such a world.'

'Why?'

'Listen, I shall try.' Mr Malcolm Taylor, looked at the stranger. He couldn't tell if what he was saying was helping this person or not.

He couldn't really read faces, intuit tones of voice or body language. He had been known in the office as a person who had no sense of humour. They were wrong. He had no sense of the human. But even he seemed to sense some desperation in the young man seated opposite him. He didn't think what he was saying was helping and he couldn't think of anything else to say that would. The facts, just the facts would have to do, the young man would have to make of that what he will. There was nothing more, after all.

'Go on, please.'

'We tried to do what was right, our duty and more than duty. We tried to love you. Maybe, you were even the new hope for the world. But we failed. I didn't really feel anything, not for you. I'm sorry. I am genuinely sorry, but my feelings, such as they were, were for your mother. Things were not as they are now. Medicine, mental health, was not what it is today, not by a long chalk. And it carried so much more of a stigma. Your mother was admitted to hospital with what is now termed, so I believe, post-natal depression. Tried to kill herself. Was given tablets, crude electric treatment, and was heavily sedated for almost a year. I had a job, I had an ill wife and I had you.'

Karl wasn't listening. He was sorry for the woman, but he couldn't understand, not this. The children, children had been the best thing in his life, in both their lives. He looked down at the boys, their mother – love and pride. The man was still jabbering on.

'...In the end, it became a question of priorities. We, mainly I, gave you up for adoption in the hope that you would have a better life, be adopted by people who could give you a stable home. I divided my time between my work and visiting. Judith eventually got better, more by her own efforts than anything else. After a while, our lives resumed. We would, on occasions, talk about you, but less so as the years went by. We hoped that you were a part of a nice family, given a good foundation in life, and we felt certain that we had done the right thing. And, I made it known that if you ever wished to contact me, then that would be quite in order.' Mr Malcolm Taylor gave a weak smile, glanced ever so briefly at his watch.

This man was a fool. Karl looked across the table. This man with his Marx said this and Marx said that and dropped bombs and better worlds – this man was a joke. You never give your children up – not like that. If he closed his eyes, he could still feel her tiny body against his cheek, burping her, getting her wind up, looking down seeing Gene there, her breast swollen with milk, the veins standing out, and the milky burps, baby burps, breaking against him…The small Polaroid photograph that made his eyes ache.

'…adopted? A good family was it?' The fool was talking to him again, perhaps he hadn't stopped, though he hadn't noticed. The man had nothing to say anyway. He couldn't help. Spite. He wanted to say something for spite – the truth, about the home, about what some of the carers got up to, just what they did. The man looked at his watch again. Karl couldn't tell him. What was the point? Karl knew that Mr Malcolm Taylor could never really understand such things – what really happened. How human evil could look, close up.

'Yes, very nice, very nice indeed. It was a nice home, front and back garden, a golden retriever called Rex, and Dad and I built our own model railway in the attic. Mother was forever buying gadgets for the kitchen – such a good cook. Yes, it all worked out for the best, as planned.'

'Oh good, pleased to hear it.' Mr Malcolm Taylor drained his cup. 'I hope you don't mind, but I think I shall leave shortly. It is such a long drive back to Southampton. You don't mind do you?'

'No.'

'Unless you have any more questions?'

'No.'

'You have my address now and I am in the telephone directory.'

'Yes, and you have ours. You would be most welcome to call in, stop or…' Karl's words failed him. His real father, the man still in his head, had broken down and wept, overjoyed at meeting his son at last. This kindly old man in his last years repaired the damage, became the dad he never had; oh, and how his grandchildren did miss Granddad when he finally passed away – an empty place at Christmas…Aye, even in death his dad was there for him, waiting in his head soon. Dad would talk to him man to man; his dad would know just what to say. Dad was waiting…Mr Malcolm Taylor was back from the toilet, saying farewell, walking to the door. The man stopped by a table, said, 'I was sitting there.' Then he was gone.

Karl turned his last photograph. Ruby. A curiously old-fashioned name that had suited their daughter, a tuft of red hair shewing. Beautiful, even in death. He looked at the photograph. Alone, he could ask his question now. How do you say goodbye to your child, Dad? Say goodbye to your own flesh, your own…How could you manage that, Father? There was a hand on his shoulder, his father was with him, holding him against his shoulder, his dad's words, a soft whisper in his head, 'Never give them up, really, Karl. You never give up.'

'Damn right, Dad!' Karl shouted out aloud. Quickly, he clasped a hand to his mouth. For a moment, he became an object of curiosity, a lone man shouting aloud, then the rest of the diners returned to their cokes, cookies and fries.

Karl put the photographs away, walked to the door. It was the wrong door. Someone pointed out the sign. Karl made it home through the side-exit.

The Temptation of Pogo

Guy Ware

Before I got this job, I was an Imaginary Friend. I was fat and wore a sailor suit. I hated it. I'm pink and round and the suit was too tight. The shorts cut into my thighs, making crimson welts in my podgy flesh. I had a bar of chocolate in my hand at all times, brown smudges around my mouth. One of the Psychos used to say I had self-esteem issues, and maybe she was right, but I think it pretty much went with the job.

Most of all I hated my name: Pogo.

Pogo's a stupid name. It's so old-fashioned, so upper class twat.

One of my clients said she was sorry, but Pogo had just come to her. I said I didn't blame her, and it's true, I didn't. I blamed the whole set-up, the system: Friends, Psychos, Saints: everything.

When she said the name just came to her, she was more right than she knew. She hadn't imagined me from scratch; I was assigned to her. She was brighter than most of our clients, but she still thought her imagination was unique. Sweet, really. If she were right, how come Imaginary Friends were so, well, *unimaginative*? Because there was basically just your fat, ugly, ridiculous, reassuring type – that was me – and your staggeringly pretty/handsome but not very clever type. Then there were a few clever ones, some witty ones and a handful who could beat the shit out of anybody's dad. Boiled down, there were just two models, really: the ones who could do things the clients couldn't, and the ones who made the clients look good by comparison. And if you wanted to look good, you could have done a lot worse than stand next to me.

It was the same with the Psychos, who were mostly pretty limited. At the Institute of Imaginary Friends, Psychos was short for Psychoses – what we were supposed to call Adult Hallucinations, but never did. They mostly hadn't got the brains to care. There's nothing less original than a drunk: pink elephants were popular, and the insects got everywhere. Our place was crummy enough, what with all the ashtrays, the empties, the pizza boxes and the filth – benign neglect, Management called it – without the beetles from the School of Adult Hallucinations coming through the walls. Not that they ever came of their own accord, unless they were lost. It was the Saints who brought them over.

The client – she was a bright kid – once asked what happened when she stopped imagining me. I gave her the script. I told her when she didn't think about me, I didn't exist. I'm nothing without you, babe. But to tell the truth, there was a lot of downtime in the job.

When the client switched off, we'd head back to the Institute, catch up on the news, stick each other's heads down the toilets and play some cards. As the client got older, the downtime increased until, in the end, we'd get recycled to a new one. There'd been some talk of hot-braining – getting us to service more than one client at a time. But they'd have had to rewrite our contracts and the union guys were on to it, so I couldn't see it happening any time soon. Management pointed to the Saints, but that cut both ways. True, most of them patronised more than one type of client. But, if the

Saints were heroes to us Friends, it wasn't for their piety or their appetite for work. It was because they liked to party.

Saints had a kind of dual citizenship: part-hallucination, part-Imaginary Friend, but way, way cooler than either. The Saints were real. They'd been alive and they'd died – often horribly – and we weren't going to forget it. They'd been there, done that, most of them had got the scars. They'd come and go as they pleased, mixing things up, creating a stir wherever they pitched their tents.

Of all the cool Saints, Julian was the coolest. He was patron of all sorts of groovy things that made him fun to be around, including circus workers, jugglers, clowns and pilgrims, wandering musicians, fiddlers, hotelkeepers and murderers. The murderers thing was not as strange or unusual as it might sound: they have half a dozen patron saints. Which makes sense if you think about it, murder being rather more of a participatory sport in mediaeval Europe than it is today. Trade was slacking, though, and circuses were not the draw they'd once been, so Julian had plenty of time on his hands. Time to make mayhem, to relive the glory days.

So: Julian the Hospitaller, aka Julian the Poor – which was a misnomer for starters. Julian had the genes: son of a duke, married a countess, poor in parts, but basically the right sort. Which, it turned out, was pretty much par for the course. You say saint, you think poor. Weird, but poor, like Francis: into feeding birds and flagellation. The truth was, though, the aristocracy had muscled in. The canon was stuffed with nobs: kings, dukes, countesses, lords and ladies of obscure German principalities and their unmarriageable offspring, and they often had some pretty wild tales to tell.

Julian, for one, had led what you might call a rich, full life. He'd murdered both his parents by mistake – he thought he was killing his wife at the time – thus fulfilling the prophecy of a talking boar he'd met in his teens, a prophecy he'd spent a lifetime of adventure and Turk-bashing trying to avoid. When I first heard the story, hovering on the fringes of a gaggle of Friends and Psychos, I thought it didn't sound like a great way into the canon. But what did a fat boy in a sailor suit know?

Julian's wife, Clarice, certainly didn't hold it against him, despite his attempt to do her in. Together they pilgrimed off, stopped for a chat with the Pope and, at His Holiness's suggestion, set up a hostel for waifs and strays in the least promising spot they could find. They didn't get too many customers. Then, one dark and stormy night, they heard calls for help. Julian set off in his little boat, crossed the river and found a naked leper. He sailed the leper back, through the storm, and they took him in. The leper was very ill, and, being naked, rather chilly. Pushing his luck a bit, he asked Julian to lend him his wife. He suggested that she might strip off and cuddle him all night, so that her naked flesh could warm his. Julian, understandably, was a bit iffy about this, but Clarice was ready to roll. At this point the leper disappeared and – after a bit of mutual recrimination between husband and wife – reappeared as an angel and pardoned Julian's crimes.

Clarice and Julian ran the hostel for seven more miserable years until, another dark and stormy night, some thieves broke in and murdered them both in their beds, much as Julian had offed his mum and dad. After which he was canonized. Which is what you might call a right result.

Clarice, meanwhile, failed to make the cut: there is no St. Clarice. She's a bit pissed off about it, by all accounts, and I can't say I blame her.

So there we were, a couple of months ago – assorted Saints and Friends, a pair of Psycho stag beetles locking mandibles, a six-foot cockroach chewing the furniture – and Julian, telling the story again. He'd just got to the leper when the call came. He had an audience and he didn't want to go: just some murderer wriggling on the hook, he said. He looked around the pool of faces and he asked me – me! Pogo! – to get Nick to cover for him.

Off I went to find Nicholas of Myra – aka Santa Claus, aka Father Christmas. Now, this isn't as fucked up as it might sound, on account of Nicholas – when he wasn't delivering Christmas presents or looking out for burglars, pawnbrokers, poor people, barrel-makers, pharmacists, spinsters, newlyweds, dockers, judges, Portsmouth, scholars, shoe-shines, or a dozen other categories of sinner – was one of the half-dozen patron saints of murderers I mentioned earlier. But the client didn't know this. The client thought he'd been pretty clever putting in a prayer to St. Julian, whose story is not, frankly, as well known outside the Institute as it deserves to be, and who, the client thought, might be grateful for the business. Grateful enough to secure an acquittal, or at least a retrial. So when Nicholas turned up – red coat, woolly beard, snowy boots in September – the client was a tad pissed off. He didn't think his prayers had been answered at all. He thought he really should lay off the vodka. He thought, in short, that Nick was a Psycho.

Now Nick was a bit touchy about this sort of thing. He had a voice that rumbled like something deep, deep underground, and he said to the murderer: 'Are you repenting, or what?'

And the murderer, taken aback, said, 'What?'

So Nick said, 'Fuck you.'

He crossed the murderer off his Christmas list, along with his kids and his wife. Which turned out to be a bit redundant, and in pretty poor taste, on account of it was the wife and kids the murderer had murdered. Which Nick might have known if he'd only hung around long enough to find out what was going on. Instead, he came straight back, grabbed a beer and told me to tell Julian he owed him one.

The murderer, meanwhile, had sobered up and realised his prayers were answered after all. He could file a complaint. Even if Nick wasn't going to bat for him, he couldn't talk to a client like that and not expect the client to go for a mistrial. So he did, and the Adjudicator was not amused. Nick argued that he was patron saint of children, so he had a conflict of interest and couldn't have interceded for the murderer anyway, but it cut no ice. He got a twelve-month ban and compulsory anger management classes.

A few weeks later, things were hotting up for all of us. There's always a rush when the nights get darker and the clients' festivities approach. What with the anxiety and the guilt, the shortage of cash and the increased consumption of legal and illegal drugs, we were all – Friends, Psychos and Saints alike – working double or triple shifts. You could practically taste sweat in the air.

Nicholas of Myra and Julian the Hospitaller, aka Julian the Poor, meanwhile, spent most of December building empty beer can pyramids and getting to grips with the latest X-Box technology.

Normally, of course, this would be Nick's busiest time of year. Delivery to the entire world within a twenty-four hour window is a major logistical undertaking. As a rule, you couldn't see Nick for project plans and Gantt charts you could paper Heaven with. But not this year. This year, if anyone stopped to ask why he was sat on his arse while the rest of us were sweating our bollocks off, he'd say: 'I'm on a ban.'

Julian seemed to have taken Nick's words about owing him one to heart and said he was coming out in sympathy, brother. He said 'brother' as if it were a foreign word that he was trying out for the first time.

I saw my chance and said, 'Me, too.'

'Who are you, kid?' said Nicholas.

I told him I was Pogo. He looked me up and down, checking out the sailor suit. 'Nice threads, Pogo.'

I asked if he wanted some chocolate.

Julian remembered me, though. I was the one who took the messages. He threw me a beer. 'Take the weight off your feet,' he said. 'No offence.'

So I joined the rebel Saints, and for a while I was in Heaven. A couple of Psychos joined us, figuring their clients wouldn't miss them for a day or two – or would be too pissed to complain if they did. A Friend I knew slightly – a union guy – stopped by and asked me what I was doing, hanging out with the dilettante, adventurist scum. I said I was working to rule.

Julian thought this was very funny. He threw me another beer. Nick rolled another joint and started a story about the time he'd got so pissed he missed the whole of Canada.

The Friend's pager went. 'Parasites,' he said, leaving.

I felt a bit bad about my client, but I reckoned she'd be all right. I told myself it might even do her some good. She didn't need me any more.

Naturally, it wasn't long before the Boss came down to sort things out. Nick said he was on a ban. The Boss said it was Christmas, and Nick said: 'You should have thought of that before.'

The Boss said it was his kid's birthday. Was Nick going to fuck it all up out of spite?

Nick drained a can, peered into it. 'Looks that way,' he said.

The Boss shook his head.

'What about you?' he said to Julian.

'I want Clarice on the payroll.'

The Boss said they'd been over that.

'Then I'm out,' said Julian.

Finally, the Boss turned to me. I could feel something prickling at the back of my neck. I hoped it was just one of the smaller Psychos.

'What about you, Pogo?'

He knew my name. Stupid – of course he knew my name.

I could barely speak. 'I'm with them,' I said.

'Splendid,' Julian drawled. 'One out, all out.'

'You're a bright lad,' said the Boss, and even though I wasn't sure he had any evidence for that, I relaxed a bit. If he said it, it must be true. Perhaps, if he said it, that made it true?

'Think about your future, Pogo.'

I couldn't think of anything to say to that, so I kept my mouth shut.

'Do you want the gig or not, lad?'

What was he saying?

'Pogo, listen to me. You can get stoned with the riff-raff. Or you can make a couple of billion Christmas dreams come true.'

Julian said, 'Hang in there, brother Pogo. He's just trying to buy you.'

The Boss ignored him, focused entirely on me. I felt very, very hot.

'Make a decent fist of it, Pogo, the job's yours. For ever.'

Nick rumbled, 'It's not worth it. Take it from me, kid. The paper work alone'll kill you.'

The Boss said, 'Make your mind up, Pogo. You've got ten seconds.'

I closed my eyes. I thought about my client. I thought: she doesn't need me any more. Soon I'd get a new one, some inadequate spotty boy with a cruel streak.

'Five seconds, lad.'

I looked at Nick and saw nothing but tiredness. Was that him or was it the job?

'Four.'

I looked at Julian. He was looking at me.

'Three.'

I could see the need in his eyes.

'Two.'

Fuck, fuck, fuck.

'One.'

* * *

In the end I said I'd do it.

Julian slumped and said, 'Fuck.'

'What do I always say?' growled Nick. 'You can't trust a Friend.'

'On one condition,' I said to the Boss.

He said, 'Try me.'

'I want to be a Saint.'

He looked me up and down. 'You'd need to smarten up a bit, lose a bit of weight,' he said. 'But sure, why not?'

'Because I don't exist,' I said. 'I'm imaginary.'

At that the Boss, Nick, Julian – even a couple of elephant Psychos who'd been hanging around pretending they knew what was going on – laughed and laughed till the beer cans rattled and the tears ran down their cheeks.

Julian recovered first. 'Imaginary?' He rolled the word around his mouth. 'I'll tell you a little secret, Pogo. Santa Claus isn't real. Neither am I.'

They all laughed again.

'But you…the murders, the Turks? The leper?'

'Pious fantasy. That's what the historians say these days: pious fantasy.' He shook his head.

I staggered as if he'd punched me. I felt sick. The Saints were real. That was the point of Saints.

'What about him?' I said, pointing at the Boss.

Now the room went cold and very, very quiet. Julian closed his eyes. Nick lowered his joint, unlit. Even the Psychos gritted their teeth to stop the clicking and grinding.

The Boss fixed me with his one good eye. 'You want the job or not, Pogo?'

* * *

I'm never going to be real, but at least I'm on the inside now, and I can see where Nick was going wrong with the Christmas thing. I've suggested we outsource most of the delivery side to in-country contractors and put all the helpers on annualised hours, so we're not paying them to sit on their arses eleven months a year. The Boss says, whatever, it's my job now. I tell him I'll have to tackle the union. I say he'll need to back me, and he says you can't make an omelette without cracking heads.

Nick says I've sold my soul, but I remind him we're imaginary. We don't have souls to sell. I still see him and Julian around from time to time, telling anyone who'll listen about the good old days.

I'm cutting down on the chocolate and getting some new suits made. I'm still not wild about the name, but at least St. Pogo – patron of modern management and chocolatiers – has a bit more class.

Trying to Find Van Breukelen

James K Walker

I can see the whole of the city from the top of Wilford Hill crematorium. It makes me feel like Gulliver with the whole of Nottingham at my fingertips. It gives me a sense of power and control, the ability to be 'looking at' rather than the object of the gaze. It is not often you get to be in such a privileged position. In my car the cameras on Western Boulevard monitor my speed and calculate if I am a law-abiding citizen. At the office where I work the computer automatically clocks me on, calculating how many calls I take in a day and deducting pay for too long spent in the toilets. It is an electronic tagging system devoid of compromise which reduces me to a system of digits. But up here I am free of the iron cage of rationality. Up here I can take the city at my leisure and revel in the open space. Up here Nottingham seems manageable and less of a threat.

When my son and I come up here to see his mother we start with a game. We play who can spot Nottingham landmarks first.

'Where's the Forest ground?'

'Where's Trent Bridge?'

'Where's Sneinton Windmill?'

'Where's Wollaton Hall?'

'Where's the Clifton tower block?'

Whilst we play this game my mind is miles away. What I really see is the road leading down to Rushcliffe swimming baths and how we used to take our son there when he was first born; or trying to spot the pub on Trent Bridge where I first bumped into his mum, and I literally did bump into her, spilling a drink all down her new top. If I hadn't we would never have met.

I never let onto my son about my happy reveries but I am sure he knows.

Although Wilford Hill offers up the freedom of height and space it is no different to the city. The hierarchy of the stones confer status in death as consumerism once did in life. There are enormous stones made of alabaster that cast shadows over the others like high-rise city apartments. Then there are the ones which have toppled over or crumbled and been forgotten, they sit like inner city slums in desperate need of investment. But just as the relatives of the deceased are no longer alive to take care of this grave, the council has somewhat given up on the areas it classifies as a problem. Truth is everywhere telling you a story; you just have to take your time to find it.

The cemetery has its own hierarchy of pain. Although death is the great leveller, everybody at the top is secretly glad that they are not dropping off flowers to the children section at the bottom. This is a different type of pain. My granddad called it the system. If the system works properly then the parents go before the kids. This way the old are always replaced with young and it balances out. My granddad liked order; he said it stopped a man falling apart.

In the cemetery, lives are placed into easily definable categories – gravestones, urns, benches, young, old, religions etc. It would seem that we cannot avoid this need to order, even in death. Yet we are not really fooling anyone. It is clear that beneath the order, chaos reigns.

The cemetery is scattered with flowers, photographs, letters, ashes, fag ends, teddy bears and flags. It is like emotional vandalism; a graffiti of pain. It is beautiful in a miserable kind of way and far more pleasing on the eye than the chip wrappers and puke which fill up the city streets beyond.

My son's mother used to work in the Interflora call centre down in New Basford. She used to come home and tell me it was the best job in the world. That she was employed to write down love messages all day for all the romantic fools in Nottingham. She used to say that the money was crap but it was worth it because it filled her with hope and that it was good to be reminded that love was what kept people together – rather than bills and a mortgage. The only downside to this was when we argued and I tried to make up, my gestures would be compared to that of the twenty thousand men she had spoken to that week. I could never win. It is odd that I never bought her flowers whilst she worked there – as it always seemed like an insult – and now that she is gone, I buy her flowers every week.

Whenever we visit her grave my son grips my hand a little tighter and I never know if he is doing this for me or for him. Sometimes it is best not to know everything.

To try to calm his nerves on such occasions we play Spot The Forest Players, which involves searching out their names across the graves.

'I saw a Collymore.'

'I see a Lester and look over there, a Taylor.'

'Look there's a Steve Stone.'

'Where?'

'Well a grave*stone*. Can I have that one?'

'Of course you can, Son. Bet you can't find a Van Breukelen?'

'Who's that?'

'He used to be in net when I was a lad.'

The aim of the game is to see who can find eleven ex-players' names first. Fortunately, Forest are constantly producing new teams as they have to keep selling their players to stay out of debt. Consequently, finding names is never a problem. It helps distract my son from the reality of death, which is a good thing.

Today it is Christmas Eve and the snow has settled so that you can't read all the names. It is time for another game.

'Dad, can I throw a snow-ball at a gravestone?'

'Of course you can.'

'Will they mind?'

'Not anymore.'

On his mother's grave it says her name, date, and then, 'Thank You'. I do not know if this is for growing up in Nottingham, for all the lovely messages she heard at work, or because she lived a little of her short life with us.

Thank you. What else is there left to say?

I chose this particular plot for her because it is beneath a tree and is usually full of birds which tweeter away. It is like listening in to a foreign conversation and I often wonder what it is that amuses them so.

As my son builds a snowman next to his mother's grave I watch people sliding about; some laughing, some swearing. Death, like snow, turns up unannounced, is inconvenient, disruptive and then gone. I find this symmetry pleasing but am unable to contemplate it further because a man has started shouting out orders in that flat Nottingham accent.

'It's five ta four, I'm shurrin the gates so hurry on up. I'm geein yuz five minutes and then ahm leaving. I don't care. It's Christmus Eve an some on us uv gor homes ta gen to. If ya get ya sens locked in, it's tough shit.'

The Wilford Hill gatekeeper then drives down the hill and starts shouting at the poor bastards placing flowers at their children's grave. It is so unbelievably insensitive that you have to smile, or else you'd probably go insane.

I know he is just doing his job, and he forgets that this isn't just any old job, but he wants to get home like everyone else on Christmas Eve and get down the pub and smoke some fags and get nostalgic about when Forest used to be good at football and County were in the same league. And I can't hold this against him.

Missing You

Rosa Ainley

I'm back again, standing in front of the arrivals board at Heathrow. I've been here for half an hour or so and I've already checked the board twice as well as the entire stock of all the rubbishy little shops. I've been for a wander around and here I am, back for another look, as though something might have changed in my favour. As though some time might have been swallowed up more quickly than usual. I'm early, much too early. I could've slept for another hour at least. Except I hardly slept at all anyway, haven't for weeks. I was so worried that I would be late and miss the flight coming in that I allowed enough time to take a short flight myself and still be back waiting for her at arrivals. London Transport got me here early. Astonishing. I was so pleased with myself but it's only now I realise that turning up at this hour means I've given myself enough time to construct a disaster out of boredom. I don't need to let rip with the paranoia and vileness, I'm already a mush: expectant, excited, anxious and annoyed. But there's nothing unusual about that. It's not just me, is it? Most people who go to airports feel the same: arrivers, departees, waiters, daytrippers, plane spotters, never mind the workers. There's the holiday that's over – more of a nightmare than that fantasy paradise you talked yourself into but at least it takes you out of the office for a couple of weeks – and the fear of the holiday to come – replay on the same theme, slightly different key perhaps. There's fear of flying (and fear of not flying where you were expecting to go, whether that's about low-cost airlines or hijackers). Did you remember to turn off the heating and did you remember the pleaded-for Valium?

There's always this undertow to the numbing nowhere, outside-time feel of airports, it's an outside-time, nowhereishness. All numb but pumped up, pretending to be a somewhere. Pretending to be a destination. The numb must be designed in to try to keep down all that lo-fi (or do I mean low-fly?) terror. An airport is outside time, yes, you're in limboland but time is of the essence: miss that plane and you're screwed or your credit card will be. As the waitee, I'm not going to find meaning in the tasks that shape the experience of departure: only chance for shopping on the ground for a few hours, the last landside pee, the final cup of coffee, check-in, boarding. That worthwhile progression is not for me; there's nothing for me here – this nowheres – anywheres-ville can't hold on to the slight gloss it manages to retain in the traveller's eye. The excessive information and voluminous space is reduced to 'on time' then 'landing' and the arrivals gate. There's only waiting. It's an empty space, a jumped-up hangar, and it's brimming over with sickly gloom.

Miss that arrival and you're in the doghouse, screwed big-time, or probably not screwed at all as the possibility of a welcome-home fuck recedes sharply. And for some people, using jet lag as a cosmopolitan sexual avoidance technique may be acceptable but withholding sex as a payback for late arrival at arrivals is something much less shiny. I have a strong feeling that being early is not going to add to tonight's sexual pleasure, and that's nothing to do with jet lag either. I wish I hadn't had that thought – it's given my mood a boot further down the hole. Something tastes bad in my mouth and it's not airport catering.

As she who waits I have no excuse to buy a crummy time-passing airport novel that I can happily consume in the parallel universe that is air travel, reasonably safe that no one will catch me at it. And I have already read the whole paper on the tube plus some other tabloids that I'm far too fastidious to buy in real life but always happy to devour when I have the chance. My mouth is stale and dry still but eating or drinking anything in a place like this is out of the question. All the tastes and smells are too cloying, too sweet, too homogenous, probably sprayed on. Anxiety makes the eating and drinking option even less attractive: still, I should be grateful, the toilets may be bad here but at least they're on the ground. I'm on the wrong side to get into duty-free, whatever those ads say about cheap shopping at the airport, but with the new rules these days even the dubious bargains that a sunny, holiday mood could transform into something worth snapping up ('well, why not?') aren't worth bothering with. Maybe I could use the time to make some calls. What am I thinking? 'I'm at Heathrow' is just a snob version of 'I'm on the train'.

I'm here to meet my loved one, the returning angel, she I have missed, and who wants to know about that? Our six-month ordeal of absence is finally over. Or will be in about an hour now. OK, an hour and a half if there are no delays. She's coming back. Back to me. We have, if my arrival here in the arrivals hall means anything, and I'm not so sure that it does, survived our trial by separation. I'm still here to meet her, aren't I? She still called me –

three times in fact, God! But there was a time, so recently, when I would have been hugely charmed by that – to tell me when she was getting in. I can't help being alert to the pitfalls of what I wish for – or at least what I was wishing for six months ago – so I note my nausea and anxiety with, well, more anxiety. My nausea isn't only about the coffee and cookie aromas liberally misted around, I know that. Perhaps a kill-or-cure shot of strong alcohol is in order? I know plenty of people swear by a stomach-calming tipple but an airport bar with its unbeatable mix of synthetic odour and chilly aircon that seems to plaster on the smells instead of diverting them elsewhere is no place to be, in more ways than one. Really it's no place at all, is it? And anyway falling off a trans-Atlantic flight and into the arms of someone who smells of booze is not the welcome experience I am trying to offer. You could say that's the problem, I don't know what kind of welcome I want to give her. I wish I could gather her into my arms and feel that I never want to let her go again. And reappearances can do that to you – remind you with a shock what it's all about, sweep you off your feet, again, turn you around. And around. No, I know. OK then. I do know I don't want to be smelling like a pub and I don't want to need Dutch courage, much as I do.

But then I hit on something: watching the planes landing and taking off as night falls, tail lights fade and all that. Oh this is better, now I've got a soundtrack. I'm not sure that planes have tail lights but they do have tails, and there's a handy song lyric to go with it, so I'm not going to worry about details. Before long though, the sun has set (I didn't even see it because we're facing the wrong way) and the light is gone. I look at the few stars that can power their way through the urban airport fug and attempt to feel romantic. But I don't. I feel desolate and too firmly planted in this nowhere, no-time mirage of a place to be uplifted. Or is it that I just don't feel remotely romantic? We're still together, yeah, but maybe only because of the complications of parting from an absence. Or maybe it was just the lack of any alternative. The connection between us reeks of playing parts – all angles taken care of but I'm not sure there's anybody there, really, and it felt so unbreakable when she left, so sure. Talking about myself again. I'm only here out of misplaced duty. The thrill is well gone, it left not too long after she did. At some point the longed-for phone calls became an expensive roleplay. How long have I been saying I loved her more as an automatic refrain rather than as an expression of my feelings? Four months? Five months? The fear is that this is not going to change, is not going to be wiped away by her physical presence. That I'll carry on telling her I love her when it's just a repetition, the required answer with nothing behind it. Once more without feeling. Her reappearance may just write large what I'm already (not) feeling. I'm talking about my doubts, my uncertainty about the welcome I'm putting on for my lost love. For all I know, she might be jetting back with a heavy heart and a dusty mouth for very similar reasons.

No! Her reappearance at the gate will put an end to this miserable loss of faith and we will, if not skip into the sunset (already too late for that), make our life together. The airport is a line we have to cross. Yeah, a frontier – I know, I get it. We have to cross the line of being together in the same country again, we have to decide to be together, here, anywhere. We have to decide to move on from being tragic-romantically separated and do it, here, now. I feel cold.

She, like this place, is everything and nothing to me. She doesn't even exist until she steps through that gate. In fact, she won't exist until I see her, unimaginably brown – looking how she would if she was healthy and happy and living in the climate she comes from instead of the pallid woman with purple-ringed eyes I know – full of an experience I cannot imagine, tilting her head in that way she has, to find me. It was the same when we met: after a wild three-week love affair she went away for another three. That time I was primed for disappointment. Had I moved on? What had I really remembered? How much were we carried away by her impending departure? I never did bother to work out the answers. I made the decision, as I hugged her longingly (train station, that time) while wondering who on earth she was. I decided right then that I was going to stay with her, to not mind the fall in my expectations. It's only much later that you dare to remember. I never listen.

I spend some time thinking about where to position myself for when, finally, she really does get here. Shall I try to make it easy for her to spot me immediately or shall I hang back so that I can suddenly step up, out of the mass of the crowd, sweep her up, envelop her in that all-consuming, all-healing hug I'm still pinning my hopes on? Confused? Just possibly.

I choose one spot, then another. The flight's landed and people begin to straggle through customs, now it's a stream. I'm trying hard to manufacture excitement every time someone appears, make my stomach leap just in case. I get bored. At the same time I'm pretending I'm not hoping that she isn't on the flight. Then I can be angry that she hasn't come back rather than angry that she has, or angry that she went away in the first place. There we have it: anger, but how can that be her fault? I move position again. I wish I hadn't come. I wish she hadn't left. I wish I hadn't met her so soon before she was leaving for six months. I wish I hadn't met her. And now here she is.

Author Biographies

Rosa Ainley writes about architecture and space. *Missing You* is part of an ongoing series on waiting rooms. Her first piece for radio, *A Trick of the Light*, adapted from an original writer-in-residence commission for Architecture Week 2004, was broadcast on AA Independent Radio as part of the London Architecture Biennale.

M Y Alam has several short stories published, two novels and has edited a collection of crime writing. He is also a researcher and teacher at the University of Bradford working in the Department of Social Sciences and Humanities.

Penny Aldred's story 'Rich Tea and Custard Creams' was published in *Wonderwall*. Her story 'Still Life, Real Life' was broadcast on BBC Radio 4's *Afternoon Reading*. She lives in West Yorkshire and is currently working on a novel.

Adam Byfield lives in Leeds with his girlfriend and an inexplicably small cat. When not at work with Leeds City Council he enjoys literature, music and cinema and is an active supporter of various charities and pressure groups. He has a masters degree in Physics and Astrophysics.

Alexis Clements has won a number of awards for her writing for the stage, including the Oglebay Institute's 2006 National Playwriting Contest and the Source Theatre's 2004 Washington Theatre Festival Literary Prize. For more information visit www.alexisclements.com

Charlie Cottrell studied Classics at Nottingham University and Kings College London. She writes for *History Today* magazine, and its online sibling, Historytoday.com. She was a short-listed author in the 2005 Orange–Harpers & Queen short fiction prize.

Anthony Cropper has written two novels and has co-edited three collections of short stories. In 2004 he won the BBC Alfred Bradley Award for Radio Drama and subsequently went on to write for Radio 4. He has collaborated on many projects, including *24 Piers* (with Talking Birds), *Wanderlust* (also with Talking Birds) and *Fierce Earth* (with the Word Hoard). He is married and has three young children.

Sophie Hannah writes crime fiction, poetry and short stories. Penguin have recently published her *Selected Poems*, and her first psychological crime novel, *Little Face*, is published by Hodder & Stoughton. Her first collection of short stories, *We All Say What We Want*, will be published by Sort Of Books. She lives in West Yorkshire with her husband and two children. For more information visit www.sophiehannah.com

Tania Hershman is a science and technology journalist, originally from London and now living in Jerusalem. 'On A Roll', which was broadcast on BBC Radio, is part of the collection she is working on of science-inspired short stories. Tania's stories have been published in Route's *Wonderwall* anthology, The Beat, the Orphan Leaf Review, Front&Centre, and Spoiled Ink. Tania's published articles and fiction can be found on her website, www.taniahershman.com

Daithidh MacEochaidh: poet publisher, writer of short stories and novels, was educated at Hull, Ripon and St John York and Huddersfield.

Michael Nath has published short stories and novel extracts in 'STAND', 'Critical Quarterly', 'Billy Liar', 'Main Street Journal' and *Wonderwall* (Route 16). Michael has also written three novels: *British Story*, *The Book of the Law*, and *La Rochelle*. He is a lecturer in English at the University of Westminster.

Nathan Ramsden's collaborative screenplay *Tell Me Lies About Love* was made into a short film in 2004. Nathan is a teacher of English and of Creative Writing. He is currently working on two novels.

Paula Rawsthorne was a winner of the BBC Get Writing Canterbury Tales competition with her comic tale 'The Sermon on the Mount'. She has since written a play for children's theatre and has recently written performances for a Nottinghamshire heritage festival. Paula lives in Nottingham with her children Stan, Archie and Sadie (a.k.a. The S.A.S) and her husband David.

James Walker has a number of short story publications to his name. He is currently researching a book on Brian Clough. Details of both can be found at www.jameskwalker.co.uk

Guy Ware has published a number of stories on www.decongested.com and in *Tales of the Decongested, Vol. 1*, published by Apis Books.

Comment on titles in the Route series of contemporary stories

'The sharpest, on the button writing you'll read all year. Route could soon start taking on a Samizdat level of importance as it quietly ushers in the beginnings of a much needed literary renaissance.' – **The Big Issue**

'Gleaned from the length and breadth of the UK, these stories do not disappoint. There is a grittiness to these tales, variously dealing in love, and fading or faded dreams and a commendable lack of adornment and sentimentality in a well-chosen collection.' – **The Glasgow Herald**

'Punchy, pithy and darkly humorous.' – **Liverpool Daily Post**

'Route is a trailblazing publisher of literary talent. Here you'll find some the best short storytelling since Raymond Carver.' – **The Big Issue in the North**

'Sharp, refreshing and full of surprises…a bit like going to a party and meeting one fascinating person after another.' – **Leeds Guide**

'This collection suggest the short story is making a spirited comeback.' – **Nottingham Evening Post**

'Some of the best stories I have ever read.' – **BBCi**

'These stories drop you right into what's going on behind the curtains and in the alleys of your own neighbourhood.' – **Bradford Telegraph and Argus**

'The eclectic, the humorous, the heartbreaking, the psychological, the fear and angst are all here in a collection that not only embodies the city but occupies the very soul of the urban landscape.' – **Inc Writers**

'An anthology of believable and engaging tales that take us to the actuality of modern life. Particularly well written.' – **The Crack**

'If you want to keep abreast of current reflections on social and sexual change and expose yourself to some top-quality storytelling, this is the book for you.' – **Juice Magazine**

'Route has arrived at a format which could almost be described as a northern *Granta*. For any broad-minded soul that cares to check it out, it remains hard evidence of a valid literary sensibility beyond London.' – **Artscene**

The Route Series

Route publishes a regular series of titles for which it offers an annual subscription.

Route 1	*Introducing The Graphomaniacs*	February 2000
Route 2	*To The Misomusists*	March 2000
Route 3	*For the Purpose of Healing and Positivity*	April 2000
Route 4	*Believe and Receive*	May 2000
Route 5	*Doubt and Do Without*	June 2000
Route 6	*Start Spreading the News*	July 2000
Route 7	*The B Vocabulary*	October 2000
Route 8	*This Revolution Will Not Be Televised*	December 2000
Route 9	*From The Underground*	March 2001
Route 10	*No Stinking Badges*	May 2001
Route 11	*Welcome Martha Smith*	July 2001
Route 12	*Underwood Monkey Business*	October 2001
Route 13	*From The Wonderland Zoo*	January 2002
Route 14	*Next Stop Hope*	January2003
Route 15	*Naked City*	October 2004
Route 16	*Wonderwall*	October 2005
Route 17	*Route Compendium*	February 2006

Ideas Above Our Station (Route 18) is a title in the Route Series.

For details of the current subscription scheme, our complete book list and details of Route's pioneering byteback books please visit:

www.route-online.com